I0555876

THE HEARTH WITCH'S SON

A Tale of Bladesend

The Hearthwitch's Son

A Tale of Bladesend

by Elaine Isaak

Copyright

The Hearthwitch's Son

© 2020 Elaine Isaak

All rights reserved. This book or any portion thereof may not be reproduced or used in any manner whatsoever without the express written permission of the publisher except for the use of brief quotations in a book review.

Printed in the United States of America

First Printing, 2020

ISBN 978-1-941107-17-1

Rocinante

Cover art/design © 2020 Rachel A. Marks

CHAPTER

ONE

For the Crown

IN THE NARROW HALLWAY outside the king's own door, Roger feinted back, pretending exhaustion—another lie—and let the royal guard pursue him. At the last moment, he spun and brought up his sword. His blade rang against the guard's, stopping the swing that should have killed him. The force of the impact shuddered through his arm and slid him back three feet down the castle corridor. The guard's teeth gleamed as he snapped back his sword and swung again.

"Your Majesty!" a woman's voice called—Caterina.

Where was the king—the real one? Roger resisted looking, but as he parried the new assault and stumbled out of the way he saw the heavy door remained shut, four more guards tensed before it.

"Your Majesty—watch out!" Caterina cried again. Roger parried desperately and slipped to one knee, landing with enough grace to make it seem on purpose. *Your Majesty*, she called, trying to warn him. Because he was the king—harder to remember now that the rebellion reached the castle itself.

He thrust up his sword and won blood that spattered hot against his face. Nausea curled in his belly, as it had for weeks, but he did not give in. He was the king now, at least as far as these people were concerned: he must remember that. His sword arm throbbed with exertion, but he pushed aside the body, only to find two more guards towering over him.

Roger put up his sword as they stabbed down at him. One man grunted and tumbled to the side, blood gushing from his mouth as a new figure joined the fray, turning her sword as if in a dance. Down, aside, up, a beautiful figure carved in the air by the flash of steel in lamplight. Abstractly, Roger knew his fascination was not a good sign. His exhaustion, then, had been no lie. The elegant blade thrust home, another shower of blood, and his last attacker fell.

His savior stooped, keen green eyes examining his face and form, then a smile slender as her blade. Lady Rania, called the Runaway Duchess for the way she dodged the king's brother every time they were to wed, almost like a person from one of the stories he told. The duke still pursued her, in spite of her embrace of the less feminine arts. She had been Roger's first ally among the gentry, the one person in the castle whose notice he never imagined he'd win. "Can you rise, Your Majesty?" she whispered.

"I can," he told her, but his voice was weak, breathless. He drew a deeper breath, and said, "I can. Honest and true."

The Hearth Witch's Son

The smile grew from poniard to scimitar. "I'm glad to hear it, Majesty." She caught his elbow and swung him back to his feet. He swayed and leaned on her more than he should— not half as much as he'd like to.

"Oh, Your Majesty. Are you hurt?" Caterina reached him at last.

Through a pointed grin, the other woman said, "Don't just cry warning, next time give aid." She moved him aside, her hand as assured on Roger's arm as it had been on the sword. A few ragged men of Roger's army regulars pounded by. A few young nobles in their fine armor followed moments later, slowed by the metal but undaunted.

Seeing that reinforcements had arrived, Roger let himself be drawn from the line of battle into a cross-passage. "Don't chide her, my lady—we each of us do what we can."

"Some of us, Your Majesty, rise to the occasion," said the lady, with a tip of her head in his direction. She stood a bit taller than he, and much taller than Caterina, a former scullion like himself who had been one of his first supporters. He had proclaimed her as his Defender of the Weak, and she had taken the role to heart.

For Caterina's sake, Roger straightened and forced the tremors from his arm. Caterina slipped up against him, her bright eyes searching his face as her quick fingers brushed away some of the blood. She lowered her hand a moment, and came back with the kerchief she kept tucked in her sleeve to wipe away the rest. "You're not hurt, Rog—I mean, Your

Majesty, are you?"

"No, Caterina, I don't think so." Just aching in every bit of himself. He felt like a tough cut of meat being tenderized for the royal supper. The metaphor amused him; twenty-four years in kitchens would do that to anyone.

Lady Rania smiled again, and the world felt brighter. "We're almost there, Your Majesty—that much nearer to your throne."

In the corridor, something crashed, and all three started, then stuck their heads out. A fresh party of soldiers—well, of the stable hands, barmaids, and petty nobility who passed for soldiers—carried a long, oak bench from one of the great halls downstairs. As Roger looked on, they drew back again, then ran forward, slamming the end of the bench into the king's door.

Rania laughed. He knew her from his years by the hearth, knew her in passing, the way that a kitchen boy knows a lady, and had heard her name spoken by any of a number of hunting partners come to retrieve the lunches they ordered in the wee hours of the dawn. Now that he was King Roger, he had the right to that name, a name that had never crossed his lips.

"Oh, you are hurt, Roger," said Caterina, his left hand resting atop both of hers, her head bent over it.

"Is he?" Rania moved in, but Caterina gave no ground, and the other woman could only peer down from her greater height.

The Hearth Witch's Son

The wall shuddered as they rammed the door again, and Roger's teeth chinked together, sending a jolt to his pounding skull. His hand did feel a bit sharp, now he came to think of it. "Come, I'll wrap it," Caterina told him, leading him down the hall a few more feet, leaving the lady behind.

Quickly, Caterina dabbed away some of the blood, revealing the clean edges of a simple slash across the back of his hand. Roger thought of skinning pheasants, and let that go, looking away. A cloth binding snugged about his hand, held so carefully in hers. Lady Rania stared at them a moment longer, her eyes briefly shiny, then turned sharply back toward the door. "Come on, you lot! Work together! One, two, three, four! Again!" She strode away her sword flicking blood in her wake. He had never seen her look that way before, not at him, nor at anyone. Perhaps being king had some attraction after all.

"There y'are, Rog—Your Majesty." Caterina still held his fingers warmly. "We ought to get it stitched proper, though, being your sword-hand and all."

"Thank you."

She, too, gazed at him with shining eyes.

For how much longer? Bile simmered in Roger's gullet, almost to a boil, and he hated himself so thoroughly that he thought the floorboards might part beneath him and send him plunging to a death he richly deserved. He looked over her head, drawing back his hand.

"One, two, three—" With a rending sound, the door burst free of its lock, leaving the metal fittings twisted and

9

dangling. A cheer resounded from the narrow hall. Roger pushed off from the wall, taking up his sword again as the soldiers surged into the broken chamber with the duchess howling after them. Soon, now, and it would all be over. He hoped down in the bowels of the castle, that another door had broken, setting its prisoners free. For a moment, he imagined his mother hobbling out in to the light, squinting, sniffing, and declaring the day required cinnamon. How many tales had he invented for his mother, in which she became daring and bold? A quiet chuckle escaped him and he reached up to wipe his eyes, then remembered the bandage.

"Come, Your Majesty!" Rania popped back out of the chamber, her eyes alight in quite a different way. "We've got him!"

Roger motioned for Caterina to go before him. She curt-sied, but shook her head. "It's not for you to follow me now, Your Majesty."

"Right," he mumbled and swallowed his hurt and exhaustion. He longed to curl up on the great kitchen hearth and sleep as if he were a child again. He had no time for his own aches: the moment of victory lay upon them and he would seize it as his people deserved. Ahead, Rania stood watching, her feet set apart and hands upon her sword. When he drew near, she swept the blade up to touch her forehead, then slipped it to the side to give him passage, her head bowed. A few strands of red hair trailed through the sweat upon her neck; he licked the sweat from his own lips as he stepped by.

The Hearth Witch's Son

Then he caught a whiff of pepper and the hint of something more tangy.

Someone inside screamed. On instinct, Roger spun himself against the outside wall, dragging Rania with him.

"Get down! Hold your breath!" he shouted to the men inside. Screams filled the chamber and spilled into the hall, followed by staggering forms, clutching at their throats. Caterina started forward, but he caught her and propelled her down the corridor.

"But they're dying," Rania snarled, fighting his arm.

"Stay." He stared at her fiercely, bringing his hand up to his mouth to yank free the kerchief with his teeth. "Stay," he growled again.

After a deep breath, he tied the bloody cloth quickly over his nose and mouth and dropped to his hands and knees, scrambling forward. Already, his eyes stung as the billowing smoke struck him full force and he fought the urge to gasp for air. His hand pulsed with pain as he scrambled forward. He climbed over the fallen soldiers, swinging his head this way and that. The device must be nearby. His soldiers writhed around him, clawing at their faces while the dust swirled its poison around them. The device, but where—?

A snigger, stifled quickly, reached his ears, and Roger shot in that direction, rising to his feet, but staying low. He saw a pair of boots, shuffling back from him: someone was still standing. Someone who knew what to expect. His eyes burned, tears streamed down his cheeks, and his chest pinched with the strain of not breathing. He lunged against the figure's knees, toppling him to the ground. The device, a brass pot carried on a long wand, struck the ground and rolled, still spewing its poison. Roger ignored the man he had felled and leapt onto the pot, smothering it with his body. He shut his eyes, squeezing out the tears. He snaked his arm down to the pot and gave the lid a twist, feeling the slits snick shut and cut off the smoke. One of his mother's finest creations, never meant for this.

Something tapped his shoulder, then slid, cold and stinging along his throat to the soft place under his jaw. "Too bold, peasant." The voice, as cold as its blade, sank among the rising sobs of his stricken soldiers.

Roger shoved his heels against the floor, gaining precious inches from the sword, then rolled sharply. He seized the wand attached to the smoke bomb and whipped it about, the chain catching his assailant's legs as the pot smacked into his groin.

The figure reeled and moaned before it toppled, a cloth mask fluttering away to reveal one of the king's ministers. But where was the man himself?

"Your Majesty! King Roger!"

"Here," he choked out.

"Is it safe?"

He narrowed his sore eyes at the ceiling where the smoke lingered, then pushed himself back up again, swaying among the bodies on the floor. He stumbled to the windows and shoved them open, one after another, down the long side of the chamber. At the last, he leaned out and held aside his kerchief to gulp at the clean air. The screams around him subsided into moans, gasps, and coughing. The bat poison would leave them stinging for a while, but they'd be alright. Bat poison.

Roger swung around from the window, letting his mask fall back in place. He squinted and spotted two doors cut into the stone. From past experience, he knew that one led to the king's bedchamber, and the other to a staircase he'd never yet climbed. Where else in the king's suite would bat poison be needed?

"Is it safe?" Caterina called again, but Rania simply shouted, "We're coming in—we've covered our mouths and noses!"

Roger ignored them and made for the stairs. What could the king hope to achieve by fleeing up? Perhaps he believed the Lords Themselves would carry him to safety. Not this time. This time, he could not escape. Roger's companions stumbled across the floor, pausing to clear out the soldiers who moaned and cursed as the smoke dissipated. Good. Roger threw himself up the stairs, following the twist with one shoulder brushing the outside wall in an effort to keep himself going. He passed an open door and hesitated, seeing the sloped beams of an attic and the propped handles of a few more bat bombs. Other doors might lead out again in the dim recesses, still, it didn't feel right. He kept climbing, his calves throbbing

13

with every step, and reached the top at last, a square trapdoor in the wooden floor blocking his way to the roof. He nearly reached out to fling it open and burst free to the daylight that seeped through the crevices between the boards, but he held himself back, swallowing his breath. A shadow shifted to one side of the trapdoor. Someone waited for him.

Roger reached to the small of his back and found the hilt of his paring knife still tucked into his belt. He slipped it free and climbed two more stairs. The shadow froze. Roger thrust upward, shoving the blade between the boards and grunting as it cut leather. Blood oozed to his hand and the man howled, the shade twisting and flickering.

Roger popped up then, sword in hand. The man twisted again, trying to balance, tugging at one leg then roaring his pain as he swiped in Roger's direction. "You!" The man spat, his mane of golden curls tossing back over his shoulder. "You stabbed my foot!" The tip of the knife barely poked through the leather boot. The king's damnable boots. The memory of wax and leather filled Roger's mouth.

For a moment, Roger blinked at the king—the king! He had anticipated another guard or minister, another man to be sacrificed in the king's stead while the monarch slipped away. The sword slashed again and Roger leapt back, then flailed his arms as the low wall pressed into his thighs and his weight would carry him over. Wind whipped across his back and throat. The landscape spun about him, the rooftops of the castle giving way to houses, manors, fields, hills, an endless blue sky.

The Hearth Witch's Son

King Agravaine bared his teeth, feinting again, trying to drive him the last inch over the wall. Roger pulled himself from the brink, dropping to one knee, his free hand pressed to the wood. Even then, the dizzying sight of the surrounding countryside remained in his vision, waving and taunting. His stomach clenched.

"It's a heady thing being so high up." The king squinted across the trap door at him. "Ah. You're that brute from the kitchen who thinks to unseat me."

The sheer insensitive arrogance of the king's words swept away the nausea and Roger discovered a hard, sharp spike of anger at his very core. "You dare call me a brute. You sent thousands to die while you gathered their livestock for feasts. You imprisoned anyone who protested. When you saw the battle went ill, you abandoned the eastern realm to the demons. You dare—"

"I'll call you worse than that, you traitorous swine." King Agravaine wrenched free his foot with a grimace and waved his sword. "You're a pustule on the rump of your whoring mother."

"Call me what you will but leave my mother out of it. She deserves better from the likes of you."

"She'll still be rotting in my dungeon while your guts are draping my blade." The king lurched forward, but the touch of toe to floor set him cursing.

The clatter of footfalls echoed up the stairs and their eyes met. Agravaine staggered backwards and started to clamber

over the low wall toward the thick copper ridge along an adja-
cent roof. Roger pounced on him and pulled him down, flinging him to the ground. He set his sword point to the pinkish,
trembling throat of the king. The golden curls tossed about the
king's head framed his face like a portrait on a pincushion.

"I can make you a very wealthy man," the king
murmured, and Roger could see the fear that edged his eyes.
The king, at last, afraid as he should be. Agravaine went on, "I
can set your mother free."

"Why would he be merely wealthy when he shall be
king?" demanded Rania as she emerged through the trapdoor.
Rather than pull herself up, she remained there, at eye-level
with the fallen monarch.

"Him?" the king snorted, his throat bobbing against the
blade with a prick of blood. "Aside from slovens like yourself,
the barons would never submit. I'm glad you've not married
my brother; he should at least be choosing from the stable
instead of the sty."

At mention of the despised duke, she grinned and
advanced a step higher to look down upon him. "Oh, many of
the barons pledged fealty when they knew the truth. Roger is
your own son."

Roger cringed inwardly and the king snorted again,
"Him? Nonsense!"

"'Tis true. Tell him, Roger. As you told me."

"Roger! Have you got him? I knew you would!" Caterina
bobbed down below. "Will you move, m'lady?"

The Hearth Witch's Son

Rania glowered, but did as she was bid, coming to stand at Roger's side, weighing her blade as if to double their threat. Clambering up as well, Caterina edged into the little space that remained, across the door from the central figures. She had reclaimed the paring knife from where it had fallen into the chamber below and brandished it now. "You did it, Your Majesty! I always believed in you." Her face lit as she looked to Roger, even as his hopes died. Funny, that. He imagined himself dead before they ever got this far. Instead, he faced the moment he feared these many months, when the truth would be told. He wished he could delay it even a few minutes longer.

"Majesty? My son? What horse shit has he been spreading?" The august features of the king furrowed in confusion.

Roger felt an urge to apologize and help him up, wiping away the uncouth dirt and spattered blood, but his eyes still stung from the poisoned smoke and he cleared his throat. "We should bind him and take him below to face justice." Roger should've killed him, but to do so now that the king was at Roger's mercy would be the coward's way.

"We've lost count of the women you forced to your bed, Your—" Rania broke off, shaking herself to stop the title she nearly spoke.

"Hundreds," sighed the king. "Thousands." His eyes focused beyond Roger's head as if remembering. "And how many bastards have I?" His gaze returned. "Same as the number of my sons. Not a single one. Especially not this one."

CHAPTER

⌇

TWO

Long Live the King

"HE'LL BE A LIAR to his grave!" Caterina said. "Tell him, Roger."

Roger stared down at the man who could not be his father. He, too, could be a liar to his grave, as he had believed he would be. "The dungeons," he said, "are they emptied?"

Rania frowned, taking a half-step back, then glanced over her shoulder and down. "Hard to say. I can see the yard. The fighting's stopped..." she leaned a little further, then whooped aloud. "Yes! I see the prisoners. Our men are bearing them up."

"Huzzah." Caterina took a look for herself, then drew back from the edge of the tower and shivered, keeping her eyes on the faces near her.

Beneath the blade, the king began to laugh, a rich and nasty sound. "You bald-faced hypocrite! You told them you were my bastard and they believed you. You raised an army on such a lie? You've got more balls than I thought." He placed his hand against the sword to push it away, but Roger kicked his hand back again and gave the blade a tweak. The king's face looked like undercooked chicken.

"I did, Your Majesty. I raised an army and I cut you down."

One of the women gasped, the other coughed. "A lie?" Rania managed. "What does he mean? What do you mean?"

Roger savored his last breath of kingship, then told them, "The king's a limp sword. He can't have any children. Most of the time, he can't even finish. It's why he kills his women."

Agravaine's eyes narrowed to slits, but he made no move nor sound.

The paring knife clattered to the floor. "This—it can't—it's not true." Caterina caught his arm with both hands. "Roger, I've known you for years, my family trusted you. Tell me it can't be true."

Her fingers dug into him, as fervent now as they had been gentle before, and he hated himself for deceiving her. All of the people who followed him, yes, but Caterina most of all. His throat worked and he found his voice. "Honest and true. I'm not royalty. Certainly not his bastard."

"I've heard a few rumors about the king." Rania stared hard at Roger's face. "I preferred your story. I admired how you told it, how it inspired so many."

Her gaze wounded him and he lowered his eyes. "I'm sorry," he whispered. The first course of a banquet of apologies he must serve up one by one. "Something had to be done. Somebody had to do it."

Whatever happened next, the moment of the revelation

would remain with him, the women's astonished faces fixed in his mind, in his heart. Caterina's eyes, narrow as a hunter's. Rania's eyes gleaming first with an overwhelming joy, and now —what? What had he seen there? He had always been this way, charming, affable, going along, using his fine voice—his only gift—to soothe and flatter. He twisted himself and his words to make the best of one bad situation after another, telling stories that suggested his low-born audience could rise above their misery. This time, he had twisted himself so thoroughly that he had felt ill every day since the battle was joined.

Caterina shoved him away. "My brothers are dead in your war, Roger, in your service. How many people have died for your lies? You're just like them, just as bad as any of them, you lying swine!" She slapped his face and tears rose to his eyes.

"The battle was just, Caterina. The cause was right."

She lunged for him again.

"Stop it." Rania caught the other woman and held her back, leaving Roger unbalanced when the king rolled and sprang to his feet. He barreled into Roger, slamming him against the wall.

Roger let himself tumble and roll with the impact. He gasped for breath, his chest burning with the effort. His sword rose in the king's grasp, aiming for Rania. Floundering forward, Roger grappled the royal knees. The sword slashed across his arm, then plunged downward. Roger groped and found his paring knife. He pushed in close, past the king's

20

blade and rammed his little knife into the king's chest once, then again. Blood spilled from the king's lips and he sank down, the sword falling away, the knife sliding from its bloody sheath to twinkle on the floor. Their eyes met once more, then the king tipped over the trapdoor and thudded down the steps below.

Cheers, hoarse and joyous, greeted the final thud, but the three on the tower remained silent. Roger, on his knees, stared down at the trail of blood on the narrow stairs. He finally dared to raise his eyes to the two women, both looming over him now, Rania's sword clenched in her fist.

"You lying swine," Caterina said through her tears. "Defender of the Weak, you called me—must I now defend them from you?"

"I am so sorry for your loss, Caterina, but I did what I must—so that no more would die."

Rania shook her head. "Did this whole revolution come about just so your mother could be free?" She choked a laugh. "You claimed a crown and raised an army…you lied to us for months. For one old woman." She shook her head, brushing her hair back from her face, leaving streaks of blood.

Roger tried to hold her gaze. "For all of us. For you, so you wouldn't have to marry against your will. For the peasants so we're not beaten for raising our eyes. For everyone whose homes burned when they couldn't pay taxes—"

"I'd rather raise my eyes to see my brothers' faces." Caterina cast about her, spied the paring knife and snatched it up, spinning back with the bloody knife in her hand. "Kill him —kill him now!"

Her brother's faces burned in his memory, among the first to fall. "I'm sorry."

"I could kill him." Rania shifted slightly, balancing her blade. "We could tell everyone he died in the duel. A martyr's death, that might inspire them to remain united for his dream."

"More lies," Caterina said. "Is that all you barons ever think of?"

Rania stared down at the other woman. "An army of thousands is out there, all around us, because this kitchen boy staged a war. Do you think the truth will help them? How much of our army will melt away if we expose him for a liar?"

Caterina's grip on the knife shifted, and she spoke carefully, as if she loathed her own words. "They won't trust him any more, and rightly so. The nobles would grab for power, the rest might resist or even fight back. More lives lost."

"Agreed. One king in place of another—fine. The barons grumble, then accept. If the new king is better than the last one—more generous, more just—everyone's happy. But no king at all? Or do you think the king's brother is worthy to take the throne? He tried to rape me the night the king announced our betrothal, and only my sword kept him off, but it won't hold him back if he rules. Do you know where he is right now? He's collecting the crown tax in the east—from those very farmers whose fields are ruined by demon blood. The kingdom must be ruled, and your kitchen boy is the king we've got. Maybe the one we deserve for believing him."

"He's always told stories, but not like this, not when lives," Caterina broke off, gasping a few breaths, "not when people would die because of them, mostly my people, the weak, the ones I am meant to defend." She scrubbed away tears and said, "He can't simply claim the throne and go on as this were nothing—what else might he lie about?"

Roger shook his head mutely. Live, as king? He'd never manage it. "No," he said at last, then cleared his throat. "My Lady. I thought I would die in the fighting, but I thought this was a cause worth dying for. I hoped that someone else—you, the village council maybe—someone would step up when I fell. My tale might finish with my death, but the story of what we achieved, would be told. That you all would become something greater without me. I am the usurper, my lady, you know how those stories end. I never thought beyond it."

"The end?" Rania's laugh turned bitter. "What about all those people who believed in you? Even the people who died for this. You shaped them to your cause so you could die and leave them without a leader—without anything?"

"Someone could… someone will, surely," he tried. His hand throbbed and he pulled it closer to his chest, gripping it to stop the oozing blood. The gash down his arm wept and burned. "My lady, you were the first of the gentry to support me, the army will trust you."

"As we all trusted you," Caterina said. "Honest and true."

23

His most familiar words shot like arrows in her bitter tone.

He sank back on his heels, tremors running through his aching body. How many had died for his lie? He had expected to be one of them. Strike now and let it be done.

"Someone could," Rania echoed. "And yet, nobody did. Not for decades. We might wake every day cursing the name of the king, the things he did to keep us in thrall, and even the barons did nothing. The peasants in their thousands did nothing. The angry generals, the guardians of the eastern realm, even when he abandoned them, they did nothing." She lowered her sword. "Nobody ever did anything but you." She squatted before him. "The kitchen-boy who would be king."

"No," he whispered to her sharp green gaze. Ambition had no place in his heart.

"You could have killed him before we came up. You could have killed him before we knew, Roger, couldn't you? Do you really think yourself so unfit to rule?" At a whisper, she said, "Those of us who followed you think otherwise."

That startled him into glancing her way, but he had lost the right to meet her eye. To Caterina, she said, "He's intelligent, attentive, and hard-working."

Caterina tilted her head. "Handsome, too. Kind and generous."

"Fine qualities for a king," Rania agreed, and Roger's heart rose although he knew she spoke in the abstract—she was measuring him for a role he never really meant to fill. "Lords know we've had worse. Would your mother betray the truth?"

"I don't think so." Roger traced the wooden boards with his eyes until they led him back to the soiled toes of her tooled leather boots.

She groped behind her for a moment, and found what she was seeking, drawing it up before him: the jewel-crusted crown. "You won this. I want to see you wear it."

"I don't know." Caterina snatched the crown, her knuckles whitening as she gripped the thing they had all hated for so long. "Our people can't bear more lies. For my brothers' sake."

Rania's gaze softened. "Just this one. Until we find a better way. Let your brothers' deaths bring this kingdom a better life."

"How could I actually rule a kingdom?" Roger blurted. "Aside from these last few months, I've never led anyone."

"We will." Rania tipped her chin toward Caterina, then herself. "I can advise you for the barons. She for the peasantry. As we have been doing. Only we three will know."

What if his hope lived on—and he along with it? Roger shivered inside, desperate to conceal it—to be the strength they needed and the king that they deserved. "And my mother."

"Granted."

"This is mad." Caterina studied the crown in her hand. "What if the truth does get out? If the barons turn against us, or the peasants do."

Her glance fell to Roger, and he wet his lips. "What if, together, we could make a better life?"

She regarded him quietly for a long moment, and finally said, "If I must defend the weak, even from you, Roger, I'll do it." She passed the crown back to Lady Rania.

The lady slid her sword back into its scabbard. She caught Roger's chin in a grasp not too cruel and placed the crown on his head. The unaccustomed weight focused every ache in his body into a throbbing pain beneath his scalp. She tilted her head to examine him and tucked a few strands of his hair into place with a firm touch. "We are not without enemies, still. DaRives, the king's minister of war, rode off against the half-orcs around the time the rebellion began, and never replied to king's summons. If he's alive and planned to confront you, I think he'd have done it. On the other hand, the king's brother, his heir, will ride against us, but it will be some time before he gets word, and longer before he can come. I'm sure he's heard of the rebellion, but he might expect a different outcome."

He had been so convinced he would lose that he hadn't even considered the next steps. "Duke Mariux? He's led armies."

"So have you." She gripped him hard. "And you are the king, by right of arms, if by no other right. From the moment we descend this tower, you'll have to remember that." Her touch softened, her eyes likewise. "I will do my best to help you, and my voice carries weight with the gentry, though it's not so fine as yours. The king's brother will have a small army of his own, and we'll have to deal with them, unless he accepts the succession. At least I won't have to marry the cad. He won't have me after this. In the meantime, stand up, boy, people are waiting."

A voice echoed up the stairs as Roger rose to his feet, her words stinging his ears. King, by right of arms—but in her eyes, once more just a kitchen boy. That sent a little steel down his spine and strengthened his knees. If he would live up to her impression of him, he'd have to do better, not merely fighting for the crown, but earning it. Earning once more, if only for a moment, that joy he had glimpsed in her eyes.

He turned away from them, hands clasping the stone beneath the weight of the crown he had won. Around the base of the tower, in the castle yard and out to the broken gates, little knots of fighting went on, but when he revealed himself, a cry arose, and someone pointed—Gwillim, the water boy, atop a mound that once had been a guardhouse. Others took up the cry, raising their weapons in the air, pulsing their fists and shouting his name. "Roger! Roger! Roger!" He should speak, but the sound overwhelmed him, and his throat clenched. They stood now in the sunshine, as free people, escaped from the shadow of the tyrant. And he, somehow, had done it.

He raised his injured hand, blood seeping through the bandage, and saluted his army. The voices that had hushed at his movement now roared back into force, and Gwillim on his mound howled, "Honest and true!"

"Honest and true!" echoed the army all around him.

He was not worthy, and they must never know it. Before

him, the king's castle—his? castle—commanded the rich green of a broad valley. To one side, a narrow gorge defended the castle with a tumble of waterfalls that turned to palisades of ice by winter. From the mouth of the gorge, the river tumbled down and spread across the fertile plains beyond, a gleaming silver strand like the jesse of a falcon set free, its wings sweeping into the northern sky. Never before had he seen Corsevale laid out before him, surrounding him, as if he might reach out and stroke the green hillsides and draw his fingers through the rivers, collect the tiny horses and riffle the tiny sheep. But the tiny sheep reminded him of the lost. Half the orchards still smoldered, half the villages lay broken open, and in some places, crows shadowed the unburied dead. His army.

As a boy, roaming the countryside with his mother, looking for a place to settle, Roger had rounded up lambs and climbed trees to pick apples. He had pumped a blacksmith's bellows and scrubbed a great lady's floors. When he was small enough, he clambered among the rafters to bring down nests, and when he grew larger, he dug the peat for temple fires. This land had passed beneath his feet and run through his fingers. It had flecked his hair with straw and feathers, and marked his knees with deep green grass. He had crawled over it like an insect, and now he soared like that falcon high above. Roger's breath clogged his throat. How could a view be at once so magnificent, so full of promise, and yet so stained with ruin? It was as if his own soul lay revealed there, splayed upon the land: the vision of beauty he projected concealing the rot underneath, the patina torn away to show what he really was. King Agravaine must have looked from here and seen the wealth his iron-fisted rule had wrought: even the damage of the Demon War concealed from the castle by those very hills. Had he ever dug a grave, or planted a seed, or walked this land with his own bare feet?

King Roger saw the flesh torn from the foulness inside, as if the dragon's claws gouged the earth to find the corpses that made it green. Above the plains circled a falcon, symbol of the Blue Lady who defended the low and the miserable from the apathy and cruelty of the Lords above. As he watched, the falcon swung overhead then drew his eye back toward the horizon.

He raised his hand before his eyes, fingers wide, concealing the burning farms and broken towns and drawing his gaze to that far, blue-green horizon. His people cheered even louder, taking this gesture for a salute and he thought of Rania's words: had he raised up these people to fight only to leave them at the moment of victory, leaving them in turmoil to face their broken homes and ruined crops?

And yet, the land still greened with mid-summer's promise and blossoms emerged from broken boughs. Was there a place beyond the hills? A land that hid nothing but more and greater promise? What must he do to make that land his own? Or rather, to make his land become that dream? For it was his land, from the loam that curved over the western seas, to the stones beneath his hands. It was his by birth, and his by sweat, and now by grace of war and words. Roger gripped the stone with his wounded hand, his blood and his castle become one. If he must bury his own corpse among the apple trees to see his people prosper, then he would make it so.

CHAPTER

THREE

The Hearth Witch

CATERINA GAZED UP AT HIM, but now with calculation rather than admiration. He'd stolen a few kisses with her in their time down below, when he was just a tale-spinning scullion, and she his good-hearted friend. How would their friendship change, with him as her king?

"What do I do now?" he wondered aloud.

"Go down and get cheered," Caterina answered. "Then take back that crown tax. There's no war on anymore—it's just plain greed."

He nodded, breathing more deeply, remembering all the reasons they had done this. Killed a king. Bile burned his throat, but Roger mastered his stomach.

"You might need that crown tax: I don't think the war's over yet." Rania maintained her grip on his arm. "Besides," she went on over Caterina's growl of protest, "you'll need to elevate her family if she's to be a royal adviser. Settle lands on the family. Shouldn't be too hard, with all the dead from the Demon War."

"Fesburg," Roger murmured. "It's vacant, and close."

Rania's eyes narrowed. "Indeed."

"Fesburg? That's a duchy!" Caterina grinned suddenly, the wide expression he'd seen so rarely since he made his claim. "I'll outrank you," Caterina arched her throat, perhaps trying to be as tall as the other woman, as if she could ever match Rania in anything but fighting spirit.

"Your Majesty!" the voice from below echoed nearer. "Are you all right?"

Roger, trapped between the two women and their two worlds, did not know how to reply.

Hours later, after the wild feast, the smashing of royal seals, the drinking of wines too rich for any of them—not to mention a visit with the physician who stitched him up and dressed his wounds—Roger stood at last outside a kingly chamber, swaying on his feet, for the moment he'd truly fought for. Dressed in her customary dark clothes with their many pockets, his mother stood beside him, arms folded, head lowered. "This room? Ye're sure, son?" She looked wan after her time in the dungeon, and she would need more than a single good meal to recover.

"Why not? I won them all for you." He flung open the door with a flourish—or it would have been, but the hinge was better oiled than many and the door slammed against the wall when it opened, reverberating down the hall. The servants' doors were never that heavy. Still, the effect of the silk draped bed, the sumptuous rug, the thickly carved arms of the actual chairs returned to Roger, just for a moment, the sense of what he had achieved. No benches, no stools. Chairs now. And thrones. "You remember when I thought you might be a princess, run off to protect your child from a vengeful monster?"

His mother grunted, and hobbled forward, her leg bandaged where the iron had ground in during her long imprisonment. "Haven't been in this room since the old king's birth." She tipped her head this way and that, sniffing. "Still smells like birthing."

Just like that, the draperies looked dull, the carvings foolish.

She twitched a corner of the bedspread. "My old room serves me fine."

"You're my mother—it wouldn't look right."

"I was yer mother before, and it was fine."

"People have expectations—"

"People!" she snorted. "Glad as I am to be free, this is all a little much, eh?" She waved a hand at the chamber. "Thought I'd raised a boy with sense in his skull; instead he's got airs and as-pi-ra-tions." She drew out the syllables of the word until it sounded like an insult. "Ye did very well to get rid of the king, and t' win my freedom, but ye can't do this, Rog. Ye can't pretend to everyone yer the king."

The words stung, too close to his own fears. "I raised a bloody army and toppled the bloody tyrant. For any reason that matters, I am king, and I will make of my rule a better land." He snatched the door and slammed it shut again, sealing the room against curious ears.

"I went to Agravaine to beg for your release. My voice was always my gift, you've told me so often enough. You were hardly even a witch at all, I told him, not like Kilsharne who could raise a demon army with her voice or call a dragon from the sky. Your powers are of the hearth and field—same as you've always told me. He'd dismissed the court by then, and the guards as well—no need for pomp to entertain the pleading of a kitchen boy." He spread his hands, the one bandaged and stinging.

"'Of course she knows nothing,' he said, 'but I can't simply have people believe what they will and make whatever magic they desire, now can I? Those who believe in magic, boy, might not believe in me.' Then he told me—" Roger's breath felt short, remembering, and his mother frowned at him. She took his wounded hand and muttered over it as he spoke, and the pain receded.

"He told me," Roger went on after a moment, "that he'd kill me for my insolence, daring to speak, daring to ask his mercy. Me, on my knees there before him. He was just tapping his sword against his thigh as if he hadn't decided yet whether to take my head off or simply run me through and let me bleed out. He let the guards go off because he had nothing to fear, but I was terrified. 'Lick my boot,' he says, 'and I'll let you slink back to your kitchen.' And I did." His eyes burned, but he would not weep for that humiliation, not ever again, though his mouth filled with gritty memory and the clinging touch of waxed leather. "He had dismissed his guards, Mother, and I thought after I'd gone that I had my paring knife, I could've taken him right there in his throne, if I hadn't been so afraid, and I thought how many of us there are. We could do anything, if we weren't afraid. Still it took me far too long to act. That's the meeting, the day I claimed he told me who I really am, and that you were imprisoned to keep me quiet. The king's bastard, I told them all." He spread his hands. "And now, I am the king."

His mother put up her hands to cup his face and draw him down to her level, her eyes soft and dark. "You were enough for me then, Roger. And for the rest of them, Caterina and so on. You don't have to carry on this way."

"I do now." Her hands felt hot and comforting and he wondered if she'd sent some magic to her palms to soothe him. "The barons only support me because they think I carry the royal blood. The peasants only follow me because they think I can protect them from the barons. If either side knows the truth, I'm dead and Corsevale falls to ruin, and everything I hope for burns to ash."

"You needn't be more than you are. It's not safe, it's not fitting."

He closed his eyes, resting in her hands, thinking of the heat of the kitchens and the hard work of hauling wood and cutting vegetables, hard, but healthy, until you were cuffed for walking too loudly, or watched your friends lashed for a poor job of slicing the meat, or held them as they shook off the memory of a lord's rough wooing. Somebody had to be more than he was; Blue Lady help him, somehow it turned out to be Roger. "You don't believe in me."

"What's to believe?" She shifted her hands, patting his back and making slow circles there. "I know you, Roger, as I've known you all your life. For me, you forced yourself to fight. That's a bonny thing, it's true. But this…this crown and castle game. It's too far from our kitchen, Rog. Too far for me, too far for you."

Roger pulled away from the comforts he used to know and shook himself. "Go back to your kitchen if you will. I'm going to bed." He stomped out, not caring that he looked like a child, not caring that it reinforced everything she was saying. Right up until he realized he had automatically chosen the back corridor toward the lower keep. He stopped short, teeth clenched.

Seven months ago, he'd been in that kitchen, grieving for his imprisoned mother, paralyzed in believing there was nothing he could do. Between telling stories to the others, buoying up their spirits, he'd been chopping bones for stock with a huge cleaver, a cleaver big enough to execute a man. Maybe it was the cleaver that gave him his inspiration…

That afternoon, Gwillim passed the table where he was working, hauling another bucket of water to be warmed for the king's bath. "Then what happened to the brave water boy, Roger? How'd he ever defeat the monster? Or did he—he doesn't die, does he?" Gwillim's eyes grew round, the bucket sloshing as he worried over this imaginary boy who was a lot like him.

The Hearth Witch's Son

Roger wiped his face with his elbow, wiping away the bits of bone and swathes of blood from the work before him. He was handsome enough, in a rough sort of way, but it was his voice that set him apart, deep and resonant, perfect pitched for spinning a yarn, and the only trait of his he reveled in.

"Honest and true, I tell you, he lives—for he knew a witch, not a strong one, but strong enough! She was a master at concealment, for she knew what penalties awaited a witch." The butcher rolled his eyes as Roger resumed the story, but most of the others lowered their voices and worked to keep their tools from clattering. "You see, she had a ruse. If anyone caught her at magic, she would—"

The sound of stumbling feet caught his attention. Caterina ran into the kitchen, her kerchief flying loose behind her to settle on the floor, tears streaking her face. "Tax-men," she blurted, stumbling against the butcher's block. Roger caught her arm, steadying her as she gulped for breath. "Burned the Amos farm, for the crown tax. Drove the sheep away with them. They left—they trapped—Blue Lady!"

Roger cradled her against him with one arm, resting the cleaver. "Shh, shh." Over her bowed head he saw eyes upon them, the kitchen staff frozen. They all knew Caron Amos, who provided the lambs for most of the king's feasts. A big, jovial man, his well-loved sheep proved tender even as mutton. The butcher slammed his own massive knife into the block with a resonant chop.

Caterina pushed against Roger then, turning to spread

the news. "Caron and Luzy, trapped inside—and Dafyd, too, all burned at the king's command."

The entire room tensed. Scullions gripped their tools like weapons, cooks bared their teeth. The water boy dropped his bucket and water streamed across the floor, a flood with feathers and blood, shreds of turnips and chips of bone. Someone else began sobbing behind Roger. The head cook swept his gaze over them all, then a horn sounded beyond the door Caterina had left open, and the marching beat of soldiers echoed through the kitchen as the king's guard returned from doing his bidding.

The cook's shoulders sagged. "Damn the man. He shoulda paid up." He heaved a sigh that shifted his belly. "Back to work, all, no sense anybody else losing their lives. Mebbe tell the herders to get ready for another flock." He scratched his head with the handle of the spoon he gripped, then sighed again, and turned back to his pot.

The undercook made the sign of the Blue Lady, small and subtle for that, too, was forbidden. "We'll plan for a funeral, to commend them to the Lady," the woman said softly. Roger nodded, a few of the others as well.

A pair of maids hugged each other. The water boy went for a mop, but he shook as he did so—Dafyd had been his friend.

Caterina sniffled, wiped her eyes, took her fallen kerchief in one hand from the scullion who offered it. Briefly, she smiled her thanks at Roger as she started to move away. Again.

The Hearth Witch's Son

All of them quiet with grief, the moment of their helpless fury passing. But there had been that moment—when Roger flexed the hand that held his cleaver, when the head cook's spoon might have been a hammer forged for war.

Roger's mat was rolled out by the hearth that night, but he could not rest for the feel of that knife in his hand. They were stronger, angrier, more numerous than the king's men, especially now with the knights depleted by war: the castle staff had more able-bodied men than the rest of the city because the king couldn't bear to be without his servants. That's why the crown tax went on, and why the king gave orders to kill. He was afraid up there in his castle that the peasants might suddenly notice the power they had. There was a moment of rage in that kitchen when they nearly did, all they needed was something or someone to show them that they could. His mother, old firebrand that she was, might have done it, but the king had already chained her even lower than the low, her witchcraft suspected, her life forfeit. Too long, they prayed for hope or salvation for somebody to rise up and free them all from this terrible king. Even the barons were restless —he heard their mutters as he went about his work. Still, a peasants' revolt was one thing, they'd need to win over the barons, or defeat them. And then deal with the king's heir, a brother if anything more covetous than Agravaine himself. No, Roger thought as he lay there, remembering the horror, the anger, the feel of that hilt in his grasp. They needed more than their own strength if they were to save the kingdom from itself, they needed the barons, the gentry, the proper clergy—they needed a way to garner support from every station. They needed someone to sound the horn and give a face to the cause.

So many stories he told over the years, stories of people he claimed to have known, his unknown father, scullions, grooms and stewards shown clever and wise and kind, tricksters from the alleys. When he served or swept in the high chamber, he loved the bards' tales of heroes and princes and conquest. In the kitchen, Roger fashioned his tales from the stuff around him, weaving greatness from the sorts of people he knew: honest and true. So many of them gone now—his friends, his mother, now Caron's family. Why not craft another tale, another hero, pluck a thread from those stories of streets and kitchens, and weave it into the other kind, the stories of princes bold and battles won? Why not a story that bound hearth to manor and united disparate peoples in common cause? He could not spin the tale forever, but he could spin it long enough to win his people's justice, to win his mother's freedom.

Soft weeping and murmurs of comfort rose from the scullions tucked into their places, bedded down on their own scraps of floor. The smell of the king's feast lingered in the heavy air with a hint of spice and orange glazes. Roger's own clothes still smelled of blood and bone chips flecked his face.

As he lay awake in the dark, the kitchen fire dying, something kindled within his breast. It seemed that Roger alone remained: Roger and his vital and dangerous lie.

Chapter

Four

Befitting a King

WITHIN TWO DAYS, ROGER FOUND HIMSELF surrounded by squires, men-at-arms, fawning barons and suspicious knights, serving girls and would-be wives. Rania did her best to steer him through these raucous crowds, but Roger could hardly keep them all straight in his mind. She steered him through the hours of court as well, murmuring in his ear about the issues that came before them. At the same time, he helped her understand the needs of the merchants, trades and common folk—people the gentry had never much worried over so long as they did their work and kept quiet. She growled over the repeal of the crown tax, but even the barons cheered that one. If war came to them again, they might reconsider. Caterina took her role as the Defender of the Weak very seriously, standing up for those who had never before spoken in a royal court, those who, until now, would not have been heard.

Most of the business had to do with handing out titles, knighthoods and various other honors to those who fought well in Roger's makeshift army. The old barons grumbled over some of this—the few of them that were left, and even many of the old barons were, in fact, the sons or daughters of those who had gone to the Demon War. The new barons—like Caterina and his other low-born leaders—demurred about their elevation, even as they preened under their new titles. Within the week, most of them had fancy clothes (purchased from the wardrobes of the dead), their hats and hairstyles were the pinnacle of fashion, and they could hardly be told apart from the old ones anyhow.

It was then the real work began: directing the clean-up, both of his own assault and of the aftermath of the Demon War; re-building towns and fields, and finding ways to distribute the laborers who remained; assuage the lords' chaffing as wages rose in the shortage; and try to manage his own advisers without their tearing each other's throats. The real work, indeed.

"By royal decree," Roger began, with a glance toward Rania. She gave the slightest nod to approve the language. Last night they'd gone over the business to come before the court and worked out how to deal with each part. Now it was nearly over, but this next was dear to many in his audience, especially among the newly elevated. "Worship of and adherence to the cult of the Blue Lady will no longer be outlawed. The temples formerly dedicated in her name and consecrated with her image shall be returned—" he had to raise his voice over the cheering—"shall be returned to her remaining acolytes, and her acolytes restored to full standing among the holy persons of Corsevale." Some of the barons shifted in their seats, though a few of them were clapping as well. The cult had been disbanded to prevent the peasantry using their Blue Lady congregations to spread sedition and plan for rebellion. Little late for that. It turned out that kitchens would do just as well, though some of Roger's own rebellion had been plotted among the secret enclaves of the faithful.

Roger said to the herald, "If there's no further business before the court, it seems time to move on. My council will attend me."

The herald bowed low, and the citizens rose, bowing as well during Roger's recession to the council chamber with its thickly cushioned chairs and broad marble-topped table. "How long until supper?" he sighed as they all filtered in.

Caterina chuckled. "Longer now we're not there to help. At least an hour." She took a seat nearby and spread a stack of pages onto the table pertaining to a disputed estate. Her partner in those dealings, a wool merchant who leased land from the estate, sat a little behind her as the dozen members of his council settled into their places.

"Have you a report about Greaves' Manor?"

She sagged and glanced at the merchant. "It's so complicated. One of the original claimants died in the war, so now his heirs are trying to deal with it, and the other one's being intractable, from what we can tell, which only makes the tenant farmers more anxious. We've gone through all the filings, but half of them don't even make sense, they're just angry."

Baron Chaussen laughed broadly. "Well, the trouble is,

43

Your Majesty—" he always added a swagger to the title that grated on Roger's ears—"they've not done this sort of work before, have they?" He tipped his chin toward Caterina. She was learning her letters, but it would be a while yet. "We are trying to accommodate the new…order of things, but it is hard to maintain control of one's own property when some of the new council aren't able to do the work."

"My lord," Rania began, but Roger put up his hand and she fell silent.

With a nod to Chaussen, he pushed back his chair. "Come then, my lords. Any of you born to your title, come." He rose abruptly and stalked from the table, gratified by the scramble of chairs at his back as they all rushed to comply. "You say they've not worked like this before—you are not wrong. But if that's the case, then nor have you. The recently elevated among us—" he offered a pointed grin as Chaussen huffed up beside him—"will need some time to adjust to their roles. If we must wait, then perhaps we, too, can be at work." He could read no more than a handful of words himself, and relied up the bickering of the barons to inform him what the documents meant. Sometimes, he pointed vaguely to a passage and remarked on its content, allowing their protests to supply what he did not understand. Lies again, this time of omission and distraction. There were so many ways to lie, and he grew daily more adept.

Roger led the lords' party from the council chamber down a corridor to a narrow stair where they must walk single file and crimp their sleeves and the skirts of their velvet gowns.

"Where are we going, Your Majesty?" inquired Lady Lellian.

"Where, indeed," said Rania, her tone amused. Roger ducked his chin, the crown not feeling so heavy now as a smile played about his lips. She had guessed—she must have done, even before he pushed open the door into the kitchen. Just breathing in the moist, hot air set his shoulders lower and let his chest expand. Foolish, to miss a kitchen when one had a throne room, and a hundred other rooms besides.

"Here." He stepped through and turned about, spreading his arms, then he swept off his tabard and outer tunic, hooking them on a wall peg alongside the tattered cloaks and hats of the huntsmen. That done, he began to roll up his sleeves. "Come, my lords! You wish to work, there's work a plenty."

The newer scullions startled and bowed or curtsied, those who'd served with him then grinned and waved and remembered to bow a little late, an offense his predecessor would have met with a blade.

"Uh, Rog—Your Majesty," said the head cook, bobbing something like a bow of his own. "What's going on?"

"Don't stand on ceremony, Silas." Roger clapped the man on the shoulder, a gesture he would never have dared when he was a kitchen boy, and this man was thus his king. "I've brought us some new scullions. They fret that some of my commanders struggle with the business of court, because, you, Caterina and the rest aren't used to hard work. Do I have that right, Chaussen?"

The baron glanced around him, his heavy features rumpling with concern. "Well, Your Majesty, we'll take up any task you set us, of course."

"Excellent. Would you say you're better at baking, chopping, paring, fetch-and-carry?"

"Chopping?" the baron ventured.

"Right. Jon, would you step aside? Why not get yourself a drink. Baron Chaussen will take your place at the wood pile." Roger flung his arm over Chaussen's shoulders and steered him toward the wood pile. "I'll suggest you strip down to your tunic, or you'll get far too hot, my lord. The wood is carried to the bin in quarters, but most are too big for the oven. Your job is this: chop with the grain of the wood and feed those ovens, or there'll be no bread to feed us. If this heap runs low, you'll fetch more from the yard above. There's a good man." He patted his shoulder and gave him a little push in the right direction. Blinking like a cave creature, Chaussen started to do as he was told.

"Well, then, who's next? Lady Lellian, you strike me as a baker." He pointed toward the flour-dusted table where a pair of women relinquished their kneading, sharing an amused glance.

"Are you just out to humiliate us, by making us work alongside—" one of the younger lords began, and stopped short.

"Humiliate you? With an honest man's work?" Roger

crossed the kitchen, easily dodging the work tables, the bellows, the buckets and pots awaiting their fill.

"Dignity is where you find it, my lord. It's not the work that makes the man—neither for a kitchen drudge, nor for a baron." He took up a slippery bream from a basket and slapped the fish onto a table, making the lord flinch. "You could kill a man in battle, could you not? You could ride for days, fight for hours, read a treaty and write a treatise. You don't mean to tell me you cannot gut a fish." From the rack beside the table, he slid a slender blade and offered it, hilt first. "Your name again?"

The lord was of an age with Roger himself, one of the new crop advanced when their own parents died. "Conor, Your Majesty. Lord of Dells Hollow."

Roger swept a glance toward Rania, frowning a little as he recalled their late nights of study, her bending close by him pointing out every border on every map, naming the counties, the towns, every last stream. "Dells Hollow. At the foot of Kilsharne's tower."

Conor's face went white and he stiffened as if expecting a blow, his bravado stripped in an instant. "Yes, Your Majesty, but we, that is, my parents—"

Pitching his voice low and gentle, Roger said, "I know."

"She cast a glamour, the witch, the sorceress, how were we to know—" he glanced wildly around, seeking allies to distance himself from his land's disgrace. "We did try to stop her, when we realized she was raising demons. It's how my

47

father died. I almost died myself. Then King Agravaine, your father, he—and my mother had to admit—" he swallowed hard, and Roger could almost see his mother's execution reflected once more in his eyes. "It shouldn't have taken so long to see Kilsharne's evil."

"I know." Roger put a hand on the young lord's arm.

"My lord king," Conor's voice sank, his head down among his fellow lords and the scullions of his king's kitchen. "Tell me what obeisance you demand. Please." He started to bend a knee, gesturing toward Roger's boots, shiny leather ones he'd taken from the king's own chests. The same damned boots he'd been made to lick. They fit a little loosely, but a bit of wool padded his toes.

The anguish in the young lord's voice moved him: he held tight this fear that Roger would prolong the punishment his presumed father had begun with his executions. No, it shouldn't have taken so long to recognize evil, or to act against it: for either one of them. If Conor had aimed his fury in the right direction, he might now be wearing the crown. Roger tightened his grip, preventing the lord from dropping to the floor at his feet. "Conor, don't," he murmured, his voice a low rumble. "Myself, I let too long pass between knowing that something must be done, and seeing that I was the one who must do it."

Conor's bleak eyes met his. "Then you are not angry, Your Majesty? I thought, when you brought us down here..."

"I am angry, Conor. There's a hundred things to be angry

about, a thousand, but when your parents chose to make a stand against evil? That is not one of them. They stood at last. As you stood with me." His voice rose gradually as he spoke, his words now reaching beyond the man. "It doesn't matter when you choose to fight evil, what matters is, you make the right choice."

Conor's eyes darted, searching Roger's face. Beneath Roger's hand, the tension ebbed from the young man's frame, leaving him taller, his eyes brighter, until he almost smiled. "My lord king, I am honored to stand by you." His gaze dropped to the fish on the table, and he laughed. "But I fear I know nothing of gutting fish."

"Come on, then. You'll need a thin blade." Roger called to the head cook, "Silas! A task for everyone. There must be no idle hands if we are to feed all this company within the hour."

As he pinned the fish with his hand, his mother emerged from her pantry at the outer wall, her head tilted like a curious bird. Roger gave her a nod, and she nodded in return, but he took note of the gentry. Would they remark on his mother's appearance—either the fact that she insisted on living in her old chamber off the kitchen, or that she still wore the browns and grays of earth-dyed cloth, cheap and readily available. She merely shuffled across to the racks of jars, methodically check-ing ingredients, seeing what she must harvest.

Roger focused on the fish. Conor watched the procedure as Roger talked him through it, deftly slicing along the fish's spine to peel back the fillets. "There, you see?"

"I see how you became such a fine swordsman, at least, Your Majesty."

"Not so fine as I should like. You must give me lessons, my lord." He stepped aside, placing the knife into Conor's hand. "Now you."

With a helpless chuckle as he grasped a slippery fish, Conor set to work with more enthusiasm than skill. Silas gleefully parceled out tasks to the remaining nobles, sharing a wink with his king as they got their hands dirty. Each lord or lady bend to their task, some with good cheer, some with determination, some with grumbling hostility. Each followed the orders of their king. "And you, Lady Rania?"

Rania stood nearby, lightly on her feet, as if she were always prepared to dance. "I can already butcher, so if we are meant to learn something new, give that task to another. What would you have me do, Your Majesty?" A smile curved her lips and her eyes crinkled at the corners, gleaming. Since the tower he had rarely seen her smile. She drove him from supper to midnight to learn all that a king must know, drilling him as harshly as ever man was driven. Why now, here, of all places, did she look on him as if he were more than a kitchen boy?

His mouth went dry as heat rushed his body. "First, I fear, you must bind up your hair." He nodded toward the auburn locks that coiled about her shoulders. She wore her customary fighting gown, this one in russet. Its hem stopped at her ankles, its skirts divided in a half-dozen diamonds that flared out when she moved. Always dancing indeed. From her waist, she stripped a pale green sash and used it to tie back her hair.

"And now? To what shall you set me, Your Majesty—and I pray you, don't make my suffering equal to how I make you suffer in the task of learning to rule." She began rolling back her sleeves, revealing arms as strong as any scullion's. What would it feel like to be held by them?

"For you, my lady. The best." He slid back from her, reluctant to break off his gaze, and reached blindly into a tall basket by the windows. "Turnips." He palmed a large one and tossed it toward her.

She caught it one-handed, drawing it close as if to take a bite. When he offered her a paring knife, her smile ebbed, and he thought of the blade he used to kill a king. She set her hand upon the hilt, their fingers brushing. "It's been rather long since I held such a very small blade."

Somebody snickered, though whether it was lord or scullion, Roger could not say. He jerked his hand away, scowling fiercely, and heat colored her cheeks. "Back to work, all of you! Our new-made gentry works above, and we shall work below."

Standing shoulder to shoulder with Rania, not able to look at her—not willing to—he showed her how to hold the root in one palm, the blade in the other hand, slowly curling off the peel. He could peel the whole thing in a single long rotation while she chopped off bits and cursed under her breath. Around the large room, the gentry fumbled their tasks:

hacked the meat, overworked the bread, spilled the flour in a white cloud that made everyone sneeze. Chaussen growled, "How long do you intend to keep us here, Your Majesty? These are unaccustomed labors—you can see they are beneath us."

Roger stabbed his knife into his turnip. "Beneath you? I can see they are beyond you." He spread his hands, pointing toward the oven where Lady Lellian's staves of dough waited. "You expect to run a barony and you cannot even keep the oven going?"

"It is hard work!"

"Indeed it is." Roger stalked closer. "It is the work that I and a thousand others have known and done for a thousand years, beneath your notice. You hold your tasks in high regard as a king's councilor, as a baron of the realm—as well you should. A well-run barony is a beautiful thing. But where would we be without bread? Without fire?"

He took a cloth from the racks and wiped his hands, then folded his arms, feet spread almost to a fighting stance by one of the work tables. "Are we done here? We're done when everyone under our care has food and comfort. How about out there? When shall we know our work is done?"

He tipped his head toward the rank of windows that gave onto the castle's main yard where a crew worked to clear the rubble of battle, to repair the huge wooden gates they had broken, to replace the broken troughs and fixtures. Through the great arch where the gates should be, the castle road curved down into the village where other crews razed the ruined houses, to fields where crops must be re-sown, even so late in the season, in the hopes that they'd have at least a slim harvest before winter. They could not afford another war, and he prayed the duke would be a long time coming. Roger brought himself back to the moment, to the kitchen full of people once more hanging upon his words, but this time, he did not speak of deceits and adventures, he spoke of the truth, and the hearth.

"The same, Your Majesty," said Rania. "We are not through until everyone is warmed and fed."

"Even so, my lady." He inclined his head, as he had seen the nobles do, an acknowledgment without obeisance. "Here, Chaussen, if the chopping doesn't suit—why not try your hand at onions?" He straightened and slipped the hatchet from the baron's hand.

Roger got back to work and the kitchen moved toward its usual bustle, then Conor said, "My lord king—have you considered your marriage?"

The hatchet slipped and sliced hard to the side, clattering to the stone at his feet, but thankfully leaving him all of his toes. A rumble of laughter circulated the room.

"Cor," said Silas. "Always thought you and Caterina'd make a match, didn't we? Now you're the king and she's a duchess, still might suit."

"That is possible." Rania's voice. "There's a few neighboring realms who'd like to offer brides for you, I'm sure, though I don't know of any daughters in a suitable range." She rolled the turnip slowly in her hand as if she wanted to hurl it through a window.

Roger dropped to one knee to fetch the hatchet and wipe the sweat from his palms. Rania's voice, her words put a sting to his heart. At times, when they fought together or worked together late into the night—just now when she echoed his words and her gaze shone down upon him—Roger imagined she regarded him with an interest beyond their work. She was meant to marry the king's brother Mariux, his heir, a fate she had so far avoided, one they both hoped for her to avoid indefinitely. But Roger was the king now, could he not have whom he willed?

The thought stopped him cold. That very attitude had been one thing he so despised about Agravaine. Roger pushed to his feet, hatchet in hand. "I have not thought of it, my lord, though I gather others have."

"You'll have to, Your Majesty," said Lady Lellian. "Begging your pardon, but a king does want an heir, and better to have more. Our poor queen died without issue, as you know, leaving the kingdom a bit open to—" she broke off, perhaps noting the impropriety of mentioning usurpers in the presence of one. "Well. I only mean you'll not want to leave the succession to chance, Your Majesty."

"Your Majesty," a voice called from the door. Caterina stood there, brows rising ever higher as she took in the scene in the kitchen. "We've managed the land allotment. Each side will have a gain in lands, and the empty seat be abolished.

That's the word, right? If we can't fill it, and it's disputed anyhow, well then." She shrugged. "Why's everyone so quiet?"

Chaussen prodded the onion on the table before him, blinking furiously, then sniffled. "Why am I weeping? Why? What is this foul thing—what magic makes me weep?" He flung down his knife as Caterina burst into laughter, followed by gales from the rest of the kitchen workers. Roger stifled his own amusement lest he further estrange the gruff baron.

"It is an onion, my lord, and it is ever thus. In fact, the onion was once a maiden proud, young and lovely." He leaned the hatchet against the wall where Jo took it up and silently got back to work.

"I tell you, my lords, that she was the fairest maiden in all the land, but at her heart she was sour, and though many young men sought her hand, when they came to know her heart, they backed away. Even a lady so fair was not worth such a miserly soul. Haughty thing that she was, she merely decided no man was worthy of her. Still, she went with great hopes to the harvest dance at the market cross. Alas, my lords, it had rained heavily the night before, and this lovely did slip and fall. Covered in mud, she found herself—as she had hoped —the center of everyone's eye, but they were all laughing. Rather than face them, she fell back into the earth, vowing that, when next they met, she'd make them weep."

He leaned in and winked at Chaussen. "And so they did, and so they do, every time they cut an onion." He grinned and held up his hand, as if making an oath. "Honest, and true."

Chaussen snorted, but softly, and his frown hid a little softness, too. Across the table, Rania finished the peel of her latest turnip. A long, thin strip of turnip peel dangled from the tiny knife: a single strand, both narrower and longer than his own. She regarded him with barely-suppressed delight. Once he had noticed, she let the peel fall, curling into itself on the table between them. Did she do nothing without perfection?

Roger turned away. "Thank you, Duchess Caterina. Dividing the land and dissolving the holding seems a fine plan. How's our oven?" At his back, he felt the heat of it. And ahead, his mother held a jar in each hand, but her eyes narrowed, as if it were him that she were weighing.

"Hot, Your Majesty," Jo reported.

"In that case, let the baking begin!"

CHAPTER

FIVE

A Gift Freely Given

A FEW DAYS AFTER what everyone called the Lords' supper—as if it were sacred to the heavens and not to the earth—Roger and a cadre of others rode with Caterina to her new estates, to properly grant the new duchess her lands. Roger's back, thighs and buttocks ached by the time they arrived, only a few hours later. For a noble, it would be nothing, but for him? An eternal agony. He grit his teeth as he slid down from his mount, nearly falling to the smothered mirth of a few. Rania's smile had not lingered after the kitchen, but at least she wasn't laughing at him. Caterina, born on a farm and used to horses, dismounted with all of the grace of her new title. He prodded the crown back to level, its circle of mink providing a slight cushion for the weight of the thing.

From a wagon at the middle of the procession, a stocky man emerged, blinking, and helped down his very pregnant wife, then a few children ranging in age from perhaps fourteen down to three. The ages presented a long gap between Caterina's eighteen years and the next oldest, the gap where two of her brothers fit in, until they fell in battle just a few months back.

"Why've we stopped, Caterina?" The man bowed in Roger's direction as his eldest daughter hurried toward them, her skirts gathered in her hands.

"This is it—isn't it, Roger?" She glanced back at him, and he gave a nod.

"Can't be," said the older woman. She shaded her eyes with one hand, her perusal beginning at the ground level, at the broad stone steps, rising up the facade with its carved acanthus leaves and window frames of marble set into the gray stone. Windows with real glass, three ranks of them. Roger had taken in the estate as they approached, and now, he watched the family doing the same. Years ago, he and his mother worked on the estate for a season, and it was just as gracious as he recalled. Two wings built off a central hall, towers at either end, not so tall as those at the castle, but tall enough for a commanding view of the countryside, the estate's lands stretching from the castle's own property down to the river, west toward Duke Mariux, south to the villages of Lord-sholme where the monks held sway.

"It can't be," Caterina's mother said again.

"Your Grace, Caterina, and your family," Roger said. "Come inside. There's been some cleaning up to do—and more yet, I'm sure." The place had been occupied by squatters, and several windows remained broken. He had asked the carpenters to focus on the entrance and outer chambers, but seeing the family's awe, he wasn't sure it would have mattered. Caterina caught her mother's hand and pulled her along. Two of her younger siblings needed no further prodding and ran ahead, one of the smaller ones trying to keep up, and a few dogs tumbled out of the wagon as well, barking madly. At the step, an elderly retainer stiffened at the sight of all that ran his way, clutching the keyring to his chest. Children and dogs tumbled inside, dividing with squeals of delight.

"Your Majesty," he said, and bowed at the waist.

"Jerron, was it? Thank you for overseeing the renovations." Roger held out his hand, then simply slipped the keyring away.

"This is the new family?"

"I think you'll find them most grateful, and most kind. I know I always have."

"Yes, Your Majesty." The old man looked doubtful, and reddened slightly when Caterina escorted her mother up the steps, her father trailing along behind, followed by a few members of Roger's court. His own guard—curious thing, that —remained nearby, moving like his shadow. Some had been Agravaine's men, readily transferring their loyalty to whomever paid, and some had been of Roger's army, like Ormand the groom, who proved to be quick with that horse-whip, and more willing to strike at wicked men than at innocent horses.

Roger followed the new family inside, staying back as they discovered the rooms, gasping at the wood and stone and furnishings, grumbling at the amount of cleaning all of that required, gasping all over again to find the place came with the service of a number of household servants nearly equal to the number of children they must serve.

"You're enjoying this," Rania muttered.

"Forgive me if I am, my lady. Caterina's family have always worked hard at their farm and the mill, and often used what little they had to the aid of others, including my mother and myself when we first arrived."

Rania let out an exasperated sound. "You're like a child waiting for his mother to open her Lords' day gift, all abounce on your toes in hopes for her approval."

For a moment, he lost his smile and she drew back a little at whatever she read upon his face. "I'm sure you're right, my lady. But I have never given a gift before. Nor have I ever received one—not until I sat for oaths of fealty and the barons decked me with their riches."

She tipped her head. "I thought you looked more awkward than usual, but you managed well."

"Thank you for noticing." He took a few longer steps, and his boot soles suddenly echoed in a vast chamber. The family had dispersed in the direction of kitchens and pantries and cellars. Again, his own retainers stopped at a respectful distance—respectful perhaps of the storm that crossed his normally cheerful disposition.

He waved them back and kept walking until he perched in a window seat at the front of the house. Rania split in the other direction. What he said to her had been no rebuke, only the truth; a truth she had likely never experienced. Before settling in at the castle kitchen, he and his mother had rarely been warm for more than a month, much less had either money or matter to share. For Caterina's large family it had only been the more difficult to have enough, yet they shared with him and his mother, sheltering them, introducing them to the head cook, and he was at last, in a place to return their sacrifices the hundredfold that they deserved.

Roger folded his arms, feeling stupid for hurrying away. Rania wasn't to know what their lives had been before. She didn't mean to be patronizing. She couldn't be more than two or three years older than himself, and it burned every time she thought him a child. Every time one of the barons called him "boy" a good eight years past any such word applying. If he were honest, it was only her own example and her patient lessons on etiquette that got him through any given court. Good thing he was a quick study. The barons expected him to act as if he were raised in a kitchen, or worse, and every time he defied their expectations, he won them over a little bit more.

Dancing to her own tune, Caterina turned a full circle in the center of her great hall, her newly full skirts flaring out around her, stroking over the inlaid flooring, and her lips parted in delight. She looked as innocent as the girl she'd been when first he met her. And yet it was not innocence that drew him, not any more.

Across the hall, overlooking the gardens, Rania walked from sunlight to shadow to sunlight again along the bank of windows. Both shades suited her. The darkness made elegance of her movements, and the sunlight made autumn of her hair.

"It's beautiful, Roger! Did you know? Did you know it would be like this?" Caterina ran toward him then, and clasped his hands. "Thank you, Your Majesty!" She managed a curtsy, grinning up at him, and he smiled back. Rania turned the corner, making her way back.

"I'm glad you like it, Caterina. I confess, I've not been here myself for years. I hardly knew what it would be."

"Our whole house and half the yard could've fit in this room alone." Her eyes gleamed and she let out an echoing gale of laughter. "When you started talking revolution, Rog, we didn't know what to hope for, only that it'd be better than what we had—as what wouldn't be? It wasn't for our own reward, Blue Lady knows. Just if we fought hard for a while, that maybe every day wouldn't be the same battle, y'know?"

"I know." He squeezed her hand, and found that his own eyes watered a little. "I'm sorry about your brothers. Your family sacrificed much to bring me to the throne."

She nodded, her face briefly troubled. "I—" she broke off, shaking her head. "Times I've thought it wasn't to the best, that I should lose them for you." The single word stung with a hard twist of her voice. "It wasn't for you, really, it was for all of us. This...doesn't compensate, but it'll be a good thing for the rest of us."

"Nothing could compensate, Caterina, I know that. I wouldn't expect it."

The Hearth Witch's Son

A shadow crossed the floor with a whisper of skirts and steel, and Roger straightened away from his old friend. He had no expectation of her forgiveness, but he found himself relieved that she didn't speak of the estate as a debt he owed, even if he might feel it so.

"So, my lady." Caterina turned from him. "How does your own estate compare?"

"I hope my home is in as good condition. I've not been home for over a year." Rania regarded them both with a cool expression. "Part of that time was to avoid the man I was to marry." A tight smile, acknowledging Agravaine's heir, Duke Mariux. "Part of it was waiting for the body to fall."

She held her chin high, her pulse fluttering at her pale throat. "I, too, have lost a brother, Your Grace. Agravaine hanged him for a traitor from our own front door."

Roger's stomach dropped and his lips parted, for a moment utterly speechless. He had heard the story—everyone had—but somehow never connected it with her.

"Oh, Rania." Caterina reached for the other woman, but Rania slipped aside. "Rania, how could you stay at court, then?"

"What could I do? If I denounced the king for what he had done, it should be my neck in the noose. Agravaine knew I didn't like him. He assumed I had taken a lover, and that's why I avoided the beast he betrothed me to. He just—" she shook her head, looking away. "He believed they would convince me. That I would, of course, bow down to them in time."

"I am so sorry." Roger bowed his head, pinching the bridge of his nose. Moments before, he had been embarrassed and irritated by her lack of understanding the circumstances of people like him and Caterina, but he hadn't understood hers, either.

"Don't be." Her voice rang hard, and compelled his gaze. "It was your cause that brought me home again, Your Majesty. Your words that stirred what remained of my heart from grief to the fury it properly held."

Her voice resonated all around him, a swift change from Caterina's laughter.

Their eyes met, and Rania said more softly, "I should thank you."

Roger shook his head. So many had lost so much, and all he'd done was tell stories.

"It is a joyful day, though," Caterina said. "We should speak of something more cheerful."

"Indeed." Rania broke the gaze and dropped her hand to her sword hilt, setting it to swaying.

Caterina smoothed down her embroidered skirt. "I heard what you all were speaking of in the kitchens that day. About your marriage?"

Rania's hand gripped the sword, stilling it in an instant, and Roger snapped his gaze back to Caterina. Her face still glowed with her happiness, but her eyes had narrowed just a bit. "I never," he said. "One of the lords brought it up."

"And Silas mentioned that he'd always imagined you'd be

marrying me."

She had as well. He'd be an idiot not to know that. He pushed off from the seat as if standing on his own two feet would steady his heart and make it easier to breathe. "He did. I'm sure he's not the only one who thought it." He forced out the words, trying to honor her role, then and now. "I am well aware that kings require a bride. Agravaine's lack of direct heirs made possible what we have done." He blinked at the far wall, the windows and the gardens and the distant hills and prayed that some great bird would swoop him up and carry him away before he need say any more.

"Indeed," Rania said again, her tone dry.

He longed to look at her, and he dare not. "I hoped to have a few other things settled before we must plan for that."

"Some among your counsel have already discussed it," Rania observed, and his stomach twisted. His muscles tensed with that desire to flee, but he held himself still.

"You see?" Caterina said. "You have to do something, and soon. Maybe even before that duke arrives—that'll give everyone even more reason to support you."

"Kings marry foreign ladies. They marry for alliances and things like that." He waved a hand vaguely. "Kings don't marry who they want to, when they want. That's not how its done. You're gentry now, Caterina. Even you might have to think about it before you wed."

She stepped a little closer, so that his hand brushed against her arm as it fell. "But if truth be told, Your Majesty, nothing you've done is how it's done. You made up a whole new story, what's to stop you from changing the ending?"

Rania drew in close as well, frowning. "What is it you want to say, Your Grace?"

"We've all agreed its best if nobody learns the truth. Wouldn't it be safer to keep it between us?" She gazed up into his face, and wore a smile like her gown—overly dazzling, a look that belonged to somebody else.

"That's going a little far," Rania muttered.

A little? Roger's chest tightened. "You'd really risk all of this, everything we've won?"

Caterina thrust up her chin, the brave face she wore into battle after her brothers died. "I've always wanted you, Rog, time was I thought you wanted me, too. At the least I know you want me to be happy, or you wouldn't do all of this."

Roger pasted on a lie. "Your Grace, I'll certainly consider your…proposal?"

"Will you, Roger? Because you look a little sick."

"It's the ride—it's done me in. If you don't mind, I'd like some air. Maybe the view from the tower?"

"It must be beautiful." She tightened her grip on his arm. "This way, I think."

Nausea stung his throat and he barely breathed, desperate to free himself from her grasp and terrified at what he risked if he did so.

"I'm sure it is, Caterina," said Rania. "But I think your family is looking for you." She stepped forward, gesturing toward the garden, her arm sliding around the younger woman's waist. "I should have spoken sooner about all the things we have in common. It's so easy to see the differences—well, not so easy any more. My family, too, has always been important to me." She was already walking toward the far door, Caterina's grip shaken loose as if by accident. The moment they'd reached the door, Caterina glowing under Rania's attention, Roger broke for the stairs.

He pounded up them, his shoulder to the outer wall as he spiraled up and up, growing dizzy, his legs aching from the ride and now from this. He burst into the chamber at the top, letting his race carry him to the columns that held a wooden roof, and wrapped his arm around one of them, swaying a little past the wall into the sky beyond, as if he truly could take wing and get away.

A year ago, he'd've married her and been content, the two of them alike in station, a good match. They'd be poor, always, their children as miserable as they had been, their house full of life, and empty of anything else. He would have married her for hope, for the hopeless wish that their children would go on beyond them. And half of those children would have died, leaving them both wounded and grateful that someone's suffering was ended. Why else had he not married her before? Love was hardly a consideration, either for a scullion or a king.

And if he did not marry her now? Everything he hoped to build collapsed beneath the weight of his lie—everyone who

placed their faith in him would find themselves betrayed by
the one man they all needed to trust. He was the king: he
could have her punished for treason, exiled, cast down or
worse. He could become the king that Agravaine had been.

The tower overlooked a broad expanse of wonders, but
the crown—and the lie he told to win it—framed his every
view. He pulled the crown from his head and held it as if he
could fling it from the tower and his duties along with it. What
a world of confusion he had won with that single lie.

"Ah, Roger Silvertongue, I have heard you talk an army
into being, and talk a lord through filleting a fish, yet the question of marriage strikes you dumb." Rania's voice rose toward
him along with her deliberate steps.

Roger pulled himself to the column, beating his head
softly against the wood. His eyes burned. Silvertongue: a name
for a bard or a charlatan. A name from a story, and the marker
of his shame. It circulated among the barons now, so very like
the names of ancient kings. A double-edged name to amuse
the barons he impressed with his speeches, at every moment
reminding the king what he really was.

"Indeed," he whispered.

"Will you marry her, Your Majesty?" The floor creaked
as she crossed nearer.

He did not trust himself to speak. Let him be dumb in
her presence—wasn't he always?

"If she tells your secret, it's not just you she's ruining,"
Rania continued, her tone speculative. "Do you think she

would? Would she lose her own title to return the slights she thinks you've done her?"

Roger turned his head, his temple still pressed to the wood, to regard her. "I betrayed the trust she placed in me, before I had won yours or anyone else's. And it was she who convinced her brothers I was worthy of their service, as she convinced so many more. She's chosen the most underhanded way to seek repayment."

Rania's lips curved toward pity, her head cocked to match the angle of his own. "You said before that you had never given a gift, nor received one. The gift of your hand— even were you not king, the gift of marriage—is one of the greatest a person can give. It's one reason why I refuse to wed Mariux. Of course we must expect to have little choice in whom we marry, but the gift must at least be honored, if not cherished."

Cherished. As she had not been by her betrothed. His hand tightened around the crown, lest he cast it aside and reach for her, right then, right there. He would trace the strong line of her jaw and stroke away the soft lines of worry that edged her eye. His fingers would slide back the glory of her hair, and dare he hope to win the gift of her rare smile, the richness of her laughter? He would cherish every moment, every touch. He claimed to have won her trust, yet he had won it with a lie. What could he say that she would possibly believe?

The edges of metal creased his fingers and the facets of

gems dug into his palm. "How would you advise me, my lady? Do I marry her silence?" His throat ached with the asking.

"I am sure you could do worse, although to cement the crown—at least until Mariux is vanquished—it would be better to marry outside the kingdom, a source of strength which might be brought to bear in the case of threats to your crown. That is how a royal adviser would advise, no matter whom you ask, and even Duchess Caterina would come "round to such a view. She strikes me as spirited, but open to new understanding."

He nodded. "I'm not sure how seriously to take her threat."

Rania folded her arms, lips pursed as she considered with detachment what might be his fate. If Caterina's fierce chin were her brave face, then this was Rania's, the image of calm she wore before battle, as if she stood resolved. What was it now she feared? Or was the mere thought of marriage enough to bring back her nightmares? At last she said, "I presume you do intend to marry. That you wish to."

His lips parted, but it took a moment before he mastered his voice. "I do."

"But not with her, in spite of all the kitchen talk. If you wished to wed her, you'd have done so before now, as I'm sure she's well aware. She can see you slipping away from her, and so, she uses this secret we share to draw from you what you would not give." Rania's clear green gaze flicked toward the distance. "If you could resign yourself to wed, it might be worth the sacrifice to save the kingdom."

The Hearth Witch's Son

Exactly what he feared she would conclude, exactly what he knew himself. Much as he basked in the light of her presence, he very much wished that she would stop. He closed his eyes to shut out the calculation on her face. If he spoke now, how would she hear him? She had no wish for courtship, even if she didn't know the truth about him. But some hint of his heart was shining through—why else had Caterina tried her ploy, if not because she, at least, suspected what he struggled to conceal? *It might be worth the sacrifice.* Caterina would be, after all, a worthy and a willing bride. Just not the one he hoped for.

"Your Majesty." Rania caught his shoulder and he gasped as her touch blazed through him.

His eyes flashed open with a bolt of hope he never dared to feel. Her glance flicked toward him as she felt his response, for a moment, their eyes met and he thought it had not been his turmoil she was describing, but her own. She released him, pointing over his shoulder to that far horizon.

"The duke," she said. "He rides."

He spun about and saw the dust of mounted knights at a distance on the castle road, banners held high, another stroke of doom. He clapped the crown upon his head. "If you'll pardon me, my lady, there's a battle on." He took the stairs once more at a run, grateful for the distraction of imminent death to save him revealing the truth of his heart.

CHAPTER

SIX

To Arms

THEY RODE HARD BACK FOR THE CASTLE, Rania sprinting ahead on her excellent mount while Roger held his curses against the pain of the long ride now repeated and did the best he could not to fall. Caterina and the guard rode with him then split off in pairs to rouse the countryside. Most of the makeshift army he had raised weeks ago now returned to working their fields, running their businesses, and re-building the kingdom in the aftermath of the Demon War. How many could even be found to come to his aid? If they knew the truth, how many of them even would? And yet their fates and his were bound: if Roger fell, anyone who supported him and his claim to the crown would be punished along with him. How badly he couldn't say. Anyone who denounced him might get off lightly—any of the gentry, that was. The peasants and laborers who rose up with him would be soundly returned to their place. Or sent to their graves. Well, then, he would not fail.

Roger called as he rode, "To arms! My people rise, and to the castle!"

Herdsmen looked up at their passage, and thatchers came down from their scaffold at an abbey roof, gripping their

reed knives in eager hands. When he reached the road where
Rania had already passed, a few dozen people marched along
it, washer-women binding up their skirts, blacksmiths toting
their hammers. They turned, their faces grim and gritty from
their labors—only to light when they saw him. Cheers echoed
from the stone walls of the village, and Roger lifted his arm in
salute to all of them. His heart filled at the sound of those
voices, the sight of those faces.

From an upper window a pair of children cast flowers
down at him, giggling and hiding their faces when he looked
up at them. The fleet hooves of his royal mount carried him
swift, but not so fast as his mood was rising. Raise the near-
finished gates, that was the key. Spread word for latecomers to
gather in the rough on the far side of the gorge. They'd crossed
over by a ladder before, with the aid of those within the walls
—no telling if Mariux would think of the same plan, but no
sense in being caught unprepared. How much food did they
have in store in case of siege? But more of his army would
come, more of them would know, and as they gathered at the
duke's back, his troops inside the castle could ready a surge,
crushing the duke between two armies. All they need do was
coordinate between them. Yes. What other dangers? Roger
recalled all of his stories, the ones his mother told, the ones he
told himself, every clever plan they had imagined or heard
spoken of in legend. Rania would have more ideas, and Caterina, too. Of course the latter would be worried over his reac-
tion to her proposal, and her envy about the former, while the

former… If she guessed at his feelings, she might never come back from that ride.

They came up the long road, the slope before the castle walls, and Gwillim stood on the platform to one side where the battlements had broken under a pummeling of dragon fire two years back. Where was the knight who slew the dragon? Made viceroy of Goshan, the farthest reach of the kingdom. Did he even know yet of the succession? Blue Lady—now Mariux—would the viceroy, too, come calling to tear him down? And how could Roger defeat a man who slew a dragon? Lords be with him if ever he must face that.

Gwillim shielded his eyes, then let out a shout of joy, leaping and waving his arms as Roger rode through. He dropped eagerly from his horse, staggering a little, and losing the crown.

"Your Majesty." Conor propped him up as a groom took his horse. The lord picked up his crown and handed it over. "Why the rush?"

"Mariux is riding." He gasped for breath. "Lords, but that hurts. How did you ever get used to it?"

"Riding, Your Majesty? It helps to start young." His supportive hand nudged Roger toward the keep. "My lord king, we should fit you with armor, though I daresay Agra-vaine hadn't your breadth of shoulder."

Roger winced as he started to move. "But first, to my mother, and pray she has something to ease the pain, or I won't last the day."

The Hearth Witch's Son

His squires and herald ran up, bowing and taking his commands: to the gate, to the guards, to the armory. "And send riders or carts to the neighboring farms. Bring everyone in, and their food and flocks. We might need them, and at the least, we must deny them to our enemies."

"Yes, Your Majesty."

"At least I doubt they'll join with him willingly. By all accounts he is respected only out of fear, and not well-liked."

Conor smiled faintly as they reached the few steps down to the kitchen's broad outside door. "Whereas you, my lord king, you are increasingly well-liked."

"But not respected?" Idiot. No need to make himself vulnerable. For a moment, he tasted again the dirt and wax of the king's boot.

"You've had barely three weeks, Your Majesty. Give it time."

"I hope that I am given it." It recalled to him Rania's talk of gifts. What greater gift than marriage? Time and trust and fellowship. He had those last two, if he didn't squander them. As for the first…Three weeks had it been, since he won his throne? He was only now grown comfortable with the crown. So soon it could be over.

A cry went up across the yard. Two dozen men with ropes and tackle surrounded the vast wooden gates with their metal studs. Discarded sections of the broken beams had joined the rubble heap, and fresh wood nailed in but not enough of it to withstand a strong battering. "Heave! Heave!"

75

Together they hauled upon their ropes. One of the lads stumbled, beginning to slide, and Conor said, "Majesty, by your leave." At Roger's nod, Conor ran to join the effort, heedless of his fine clothes, an extra set of hands to the necessary work. His vision of the kingdom come to life: knights, masons, lords and stable hands side by side and hands to the work.

"At's a good one, eh?" His mother mounted the steps, taking each slowly and heaving herself up. "One o' them boys came in, saying ye needed something for pain."

"Horseback riding shall be the death of me." Meant in jest, the statement struck him cold. Lords willing he'd live so long as to die that way. "Have you heard? Duke Mariux could be here as soon as sundown."

"Cor, then we've plenty of time." She waggled a bottle at him. "Drink some of this, should dull the edge a bit, and we'll get moving."

"Plenty?" He swirled the liquid and tossed back a bitter swallow. "At least we'll get the gates up and the local citizens inside the walls. Maybe add a few dozen—"

She punched his arm. "Ye don't mean to fight the rightful heir?" At least she had lowered her voice to a whisper.

Roger shook his head, the crown weighing down his hair. "Rightful? The tyrant's brother, renowned for his similar cruelty. Royal blood he may have, but it's hard to see the right in that." He pushed the bottle back into her hands and walked away, feeling, too, the weight of the story he had claimed. The Rightful Heir come to expel the Usurper. But today, the usurper was him.

Across the yard clustered the useful structures of royalty: the stables for his horses, the smithy for his arms, the mews for his hawks and falcons. As a scullion, one of his favorite duties had been to feed the falcons when the weather prevented the falconers from taking them hunting. They were fast, but lazy, preferring to snatch meat from a hand than to snatch targets from the sky. He hoped to learn to hunt with them himself—if he survived. By the wall, a cheer rose up as the gates once more occupied their frame. One stood closed now, leaving a long half-arch of sunlight where a silhouetted rider stretched out toward him as a regiment approached. The leader trotted, her hair bouncing on her shoulders, her skirts flaring at the horse's sides, and at her back two dozen more troops, mostly knights from a division sent to rout a bandit's gang from the nearby hills. Rania had ridden out to bring them home.

Roger smiled to himself as he continued on his path. Every person who came through that gate, armed and ready to defend the dream brought with them a boon of hope that strengthened him. The bows, the curtsies, the cheers and the flowers, the way their faces lifted and eyes brightened made him walk taller, hold tighter to the damnable crown. What could they not do if their hearts and hands were willing?

Smoke billowed from the forges where the armorers worked, hammering the dents from the kettles they needed to feed the new arrivals, repairing the bars for the great gate, their labor unhurried with the efficient movements of long practice. The smell of the smithy tingled his nostrils with iron and coal. One of the men stepped aside, and, hearing what he needed, brought him to the stores where the castle's armor was kept. The king's breastplate cut at his chest, and must be rejected. The armorer sighed. "Your Majesty, you should've let us work on this before now. You were bound to need it one day."

"Fixing the gates and the cauldrons took precedence. All else fails, I'll just wear a pot on my head."

The armorer gave a gap-toothed grin. "Aye, Your Majesty. 'Til all are warmed and fed, isn't that your words?"

Warmth rushed him then, and he thought perhaps he could be fed on that alone. "They are, my friend. If not the breastplate, what else?"

They found a shirt of mail with buckles made for a man of greater girth, but it would do. The king's gilded gorget defended his throat and the king's crown-topped helm would surmount the lot. Thick leather gauntlets, greaves for his legs where the mail ended. By now, his squires attended him, helping him on with the quilted armoring shirt and everything else on top. It stifled him from chin to ankle to fingertips. Last of all, the belt of gold and silver bosses, and the straps that held his sword. He lifted his arms out of the way, turning as they worked. Rania strolled past the wide open door.

"You've seen the army?" he called to her. "How many has Mariux?"

"About three hundred." She added softly, without his

asking, "And we've got maybe half that, many of whom aren't warriors."

Roger nodded his thanks. Half so many, and a broken castle. "More will come to the muster point in the hills, if we can coordinate with them we might divide the duke's attentions."

"Roger!" Caterina rode through the open side of the gate and straight toward him, sending Rania back a few steps. "At the mill. Look what they've made." She gestured toward a laden pack horse. The man walking with it tugged free one end of a cloth bundle, revealing the sleek points of a dozen bows. "Arrows, too!"

"Most of the knights can pull a bow, the huntsmen, too, and the poachers, even," Rania said. "That's perfect."

"Your Grace, can you see they're distributed?"

"Of course." Caterina hopped down from her horse and led it toward the stables as the grooms hurried out to meet her.

"Lady Rania, would you muster the ground troops? I've sent word how to manage the fight if it comes within, but there's no telling if they've taken it to heart. And Rania—"

A tilt of her head, listening as if whatever he said next could be the most important words ever spoken. "I want you at the back, with the castle defenses."

Her face hardened, her hand gripping her sword hilt. "But my lord king—"

Roger dropped his voice to a murmur, searching her face. "What will he do to you if he catches you, my lady? I

79

should prefer to delay that for as long as possible."

She wavered, a hint of white edging her eyes. "As would I, Your Majesty." She swept her sword up, then aside in a dangerous salute, and moved away.

Atop the gate, Gwillim blasted a horn, three short bleats like a frightened goat. Here it came. Wiping his hands and straightening his soiled jerkin, Conor hurried toward Roger, and from the castle came Baron Chaussen with the butcher at his side, summoned from the hall. His court collected around him. For a long moment, sunlight from the half-open door streamed golden across them all, then his men heaved the gate to and plunged them into shadow.

Chapter

Seven

Heir Apparent

BEYOND THE GATE, THE TRUMPETS DREW NEARER, with the sound of tramping feet, then a powerful voice calling the halt. Roger and Conor shared a look, and Roger forced himself to breathe deeply, filling his chest beneath the weight of mail.

"Unto the usurper, Roger Silvertongue, does the rightful heir Mariux, Duke of Denneton, issue this word," cried a voice outside the gates. "We are come in righteous anger to the gates of the castle that should be ours. We will give you this single chance for parley, under the flag of peace. Come forth and let us share council."

The butcher snorted. "Not bloody likely."

Roger planted the helmet on his head. "Will you men come with me to lay eyes upon the enemy?"

"Of course, Sire." Conor stepped up, pulling on a metal

skullcap with a cowl of chainmail that protected his throat.

"You're not going out there?" Caterina demanded.

He shook his head, the helm feeling like a cage that echoed the pulsing of his skull. "Up to the tower. I am king in my own castle. The gates open on my command."

The butcher pulled on an older helm from the castle armory. "Ought to be Caterina, going with you but she's unarmed," he said, and she nodded. She toyed with the kerchief she kept in her sleeve, tugging it forward, tucking it back.

Roger remembered the first time he was a king in his own castle, after he slew Agravaine and admitted to his lie. He could almost see the moment reflected in her gaze. "It's just a parley, Caterina," Roger assured her. He touched her shoulder, his gauntlet looking huge and warlike beside the flowered embroidery of her bodice. "A chance to exchange threats and bluffs and try to convince the other to back down. As we did with Agravaine before." When they had been outside the gates in a large enough force to make even that proud king pay attention to a rabble of peasants and rebel lords.

"You'll be good at it, then, not that he listened." She mustered a brave smile.

"A tyrant never looks to give up the throne, Your Grace," Conor said. "Can't bear to let loose the reins of power or the spoils he wrings from his own people."

"Come, Your Grace, let's see to the defenses." Chaussen beckoned Caterina, and the two of them went quietly to work.

The Hearth Witch's Son

With his small entourage, Roger approached the gate tower and mounted the steps. The top course of stonework had broken in the Demon War and now formed the base of the rubble heap just inside the wall. Had they catapults, they could be launching those stones against their enemies. The steps wound upward two levels, to the broken section where Gwillim and two soldiers sheltered behind the partial wall that remained, along with his own herald, prepared to answer to their enemy. All made brief acknowledgments of Roger's presence.

The first time Roger looked out from a castle tower, he saw the beauty of his wounded land spread before him and swore an oath within his heart that if he must live as king, then he would strive to be a good one, a steward to his country, and a shepherd to his people. Now, he saw only the shadows cast upon that dream. The sun gleamed low over the western hills, staining their slopes with blood. Before the wall, at a calculated distance beyond bowshot armored knights sat their horses, reflecting the sun's red glory. Arrayed behind them in careful ranks stood crossbowmen, pike men, men at arms. At the back, a rank of men set tents and laid fires, preparing their camp. Three hundred men ready to break down his gate and slaughter his people. Two heralds stood forth, one with the trumpet, the other with a flag of parley.

Toward the front, on a tall bay steed sat the duke himself, fully armored in steel etched with his arms, and already differenced with the crown he claimed. A sword hung

in his hand, and two mounted knights held banners of his
duchy and of Corsevale itself, a match to the king's banners
that flew from Roger's own towers. For himself, he had no
device, no mark of chivalry. Roger stood taller, projecting
himself the king that he had claimed. He pitched his voice for
depth and resonance. "Who dares the king's gate with such
bold words?"

The duke's helmeted head lifted as he aimed his gaze
skyward. "Step aside," he growled. He kneed his horse to urge
his heralds out of the way, one man dodging and nearly falling
on the beaten road. "Can that be the usurper himself? Can he
be so cocksure as to show his face above my property, wearing
the helm that should be mine? You, knave, have slain my
brother who named me his heir. I say you have no right to the
crown or to the keep, and I shall avenge myself upon you!"

"Your Grace, he is the son of Agravaine himself, and
king by right of arms," answered Roger's own herald.

Mariux laughed. He snorted with laughter. His shoulders
shook with it, rattling his steel. "Is that his claim? Is that what
he's told you all?" Mariux swung his sword up, aiming it at
Roger. "He claims to be the son of Agravaine, but he is none!
My brother had no sons, nor daughters either—he had no
issue."

"None save me," Roger answered. "A bastard in birth, but
noble in bearing. It's only recently I learned the story of my
own birth, when he imprisoned my mother in the hopes of
preventing my rise. As you can see, Your Grace, he failed. I

have risen." Roger spread his arms, catching the gold of the setting sun against his chest and letting it warm his face. "He had no issue, you say—perhaps not with others, but my mother has certain herbs and talents, and it was thus that she was able to carry his child. She concealed me, Your Grace, for fear of your fury in your dispossession."

"You lying swine!" Mariux pointed his sword back and his troops parted, leading for a small group. Two women, one elderly, and a man in a doctor's robe. "I bring before you the first of many witnesses that what I say is true. It grieves me to speak so plainly of the beloved dead, but Agravaine would rather the truth be told and his usurper cast down than to go to the sacred Lords unavenged."

Witnesses? Blue Lady. Roger's heart drained into his feet, the crown on his helm growing heavier by the moment. "What folly have you, Your Grace? Whom have you paid to tell tales on your behalf?"

"We should slay him now," the butcher said. "Such nonsense."

At the wall beside him, a soldier readied his bow. "Say the word, Your Majesty," he murmured, and Roger almost wished he'd already said it, but he would not be the one to break the parley with violence. Better to stand in confidence than to hide in violence.

"My brother let out that it was his beloved wife, our dear queen, who could bear no children, but I have here her own nursemaid in whom she confided, and who, in her youth, once brought her certain herbs to cleanse her womb of a child unlawfully conceived. I have here, as well, a prostitute of the city of Gylfyn with whom the king visited on a sojourn there, and, too, the physician who attended him in his youth. Both will attest to a singular truth, one the king had been known to keep silent by a means most ruthless." After making this dramatic declaration, Mariux paused, and Roger had the awful feeling he confronted now a liar even more skilled than himself. Or else, at last, he faced the truth.

"King Agravaine had a dread secret," Mariux continued. "He and I were out riding in our youth when we startled up an orc out raiding. We gave chase, of course, and Agravaine was fallen. During the fall or during the fight, he took a most grievous wound, and this physician attended him, and informed him that he should never sire children. Only a handful of people ever knew, and they either lived in silence or died in it. This kitchen boy is a liar and a coward!"

"No!" Gwillim shouted, but the duke hadn't finished yet.

"All you who cringe inside that castle—my castle—I give you until tonight to open these gates and deliver his head! If you fail in this by dawn, I and my men shall break these gates and take the head of every man, woman, and child who shelters there, saving only my promised bride. The choice is yours —the head should be his."

The duke spurred his horse to rear. He spun about, and his heralds again scattered.

"He's dropped the parley flag," the butcher cried, and the

soldier loosed an arrow that skipped harmlessly from the armor of one of the duke's guards.

In answer, the crossbows fired their response. Roger leapt toward the wall, flinging Gwillim down behind it. Bolts skittered against the stones around him and someone yelled. His herald tumbled in a streak of blood. Roger grabbed the man, shielding him with his own hunched body. "Down! Gwillim, go!"

The butcher and the boy hurried down the stairs, the soldier standing with his back to the only bit of wall tall enough to defend him.

"Your Majesty, are you hurt?" Conor knelt beside him, holding up a shield at their backs

"It's the herald." Roger stripped off the gauntlets that made him clumsy and gathered the injured man to his chest.

"Go, Your Majesty." Conor helped him up and watched his back as he hurried down the stairs, calling for the surgeons.

By the time they arrived, breathless, three men met them, taking the wounded herald from Roger's arms and bearing him off.

Roger stripped off his helmet and shook back his hair, sweat already slicking his brow. "I need two more men up those stairs—armored. We need a barricade up there as well, something to defend the soldiers from those accursed crossbows. I want the carpenters on it right away." He had his people working on the castle to defend them as well as the farms and orchards to feed them. They were too few and spread too thin. At least they were unlikely to expect an attack tonight—perhaps they should be planning one. His body servants trotted up with the crown on its velvet pillow. He replaced it on his head, a gesture almost natural now, though the boys stared up at him more openly than usual. Had they heard the threat to kill them all? Nobody moved for the stairs, nor did the carpenters fall out from their posts to take up their tools. Roger's innards turned to ice as twisted and fragile as winter's touch upon the waterfalls. The herald's blood seeped from ring to ring along his mail.

He swung about, locating the butcher and pinning him with a glare. "First shot tonight should not have been ours. The parley flag was dropped when he ran down his own man, it wasn't lowered with intention. Let our enemy reveal himself for a cad—there's no need for us to demean ourselves. Let us not forget that our cause is justice, whether for a scullion or a lord."

The butcher, too, removed his helmet and let it drop from his hand. The helmet's fall rang into a spreading silence from the gates, eyes raised to Roger, then sliding away. Sweaty hands fidgeting on their weapons, lips compressed and knuckles whitened. Gone was the bravado that had carried him up those stairs. The butcher weighed his cleaver in his hands. "Is it true? What he said about the king—about you?"

Roger recoiled. The thought of defending the lie sickened him but how should he now give up the truth? He turned his denial into a question. "You believed him? How long have I known you?"

"Would he really kill all of us?" Gwillim said, shivering and suddenly much younger than his twelve years.

"Of course his threats frighten you—they're meant to. He wants us to imagine our defeat instead of his own."

Chaussen and Caterina slowed as they came up along the path between the rubble and the wall, and the baron's brows worked. "The duke's his own brother," said Chaussen. "I don't think he's enough imagination to invent such a yarn, and find the people to back it up, a doctor, a nurse, a whore?"

"Do you doubt the king?" Conor replied. "Mariux has plenty of reason to lie, and plenty of money to pay others for lies of their own."

"My friends," Roger said, "we knew he'd ride against us, that he would try to divide us—don't let it work. Don't give in to that temptation, or we are lost. If we stand strong and stand together, we can—"

"You're not denying it," Chaussen interrupted. "Are you? Are you no more than a fraud—a kitchen boy who's set to get us all killed?" He turned his sword on Roger, who leapt back, fumbling for his own blade. The red fury of the baron's face glowed before him. The words rushed like a wave through the crowd, faces turning toward him, weapons that should be aimed at their enemies swaying with concern.

"My friends, please." Roger spread his hands. Their attention usually filled him with strength and the sense of their collective will. Their expressions now ranged from dismay to confusion to anger. The restive murmur rose like a beehive disturbed. Caterina stood stiffly just behind Chaussen, her hands clenched into her skirts, her eyes aimed at Roger. He longed to scan the crowd for Rania, for any friendly face, but he dare not look away. "He wants to us to fight amongst ourselves. Why else would he say all of that? It means he's afraid. He knows we can defeat him." He struggled to control his voice. If he could woo them back, echo the strength they so often gave to him, surely they could unite once more. "If he thought he would win, why bother with talking?"

"But what if it's true? Why should we follow a usurper when our allegiance belongs to the heir, the one Agravaine himself selected." Chaussen insisted. "Say it, Your Majesty—" and the jibe that always edged the title on his lips became a sneer.

"It's a lie." Conor's sword swished free and he stepped up to Roger's side. "Have at you, Chaussen, if you believe the ass outside the gate. You know what he is, what he's like—he'd say anything to steal the throne."

"How, sir, from one who's already stolen it?" Chaussen lunged and Conor parried.

Roger's heart thundered, rocked by the knowledge that one, at least stood by him, and hearing the murmurs of assent that echoed Conor's words. And yet, it was no lie, a fact that clenched his stomach. Could he let Conor defend for his honor when he had none? When too many had already died for his lie? "This must stop! We cannot afford to fight each other. My lords, no more."

Fear unraveled the forces he had brought together, doubt separating lords from scullions from laborers from knights.

Conor and Chaussen circled, clashed and parted. Roger lifted his own blade as he sought an opening to part them. Conor lunged and Chaussen stumbled. Three wobbling steps. His sword arm smacked the heap of rubble and he cried out, the blade knocked from his grip. He slipped, dodging Conor's slash by accident. Chaussen rolled and Conor pounced after him. Let them go, let Conor win and prove the truth with steel.

"No!" Roger roared. "My lord, hold your blow!" He leapt between them. Conor's blade clanged against his own, sending a shock down his bones as if he should be shattered by the blow.

Across their locked blades, Conor's lean face set into grim lines. "Is it true, Your Majesty? Why should you defend him from a lie?"

Let Conor be a killer and carry that weight upon his soul. When the truth came clear, when the witnesses mounted, how then would Conor ever live with this day? Roger could not do it. One thing to slay an enemy in righteous battle, for the freedom of all, another to kill your ally for knowing the truth. Roger drew back his arm, and no power of his could recall his hesitation to speak some denial and reclaim his own lie.

Conor's lips parted and his eyes blurred with pain. "No," he mouthed. He stumbled back leaving Roger unsteady, his feet braced to defend a man he didn't even like from a man he claimed a friend.

"Is it true? Who are you?" The butcher hollered.

"Why does it matter?" Roger answered. "Are your lives not better now? Have we not won and begun a kingdom worth preserving? Is it only blood that earns a crown? Of course you are afraid, but don't let fear stop you from doing what's right."

His backers and his accusers parted, clearing the ground where he stood, the ground that was already crumbling beneath his feet. Chaussen slowly rose, dusting himself off, and Roger surveyed the crowd around him.

Where before there had been muttering, confusion and concern, now he stood at the center of a spreading ring of silence. Caterina stepped up before him. Tears gleamed in her eyes, and she whispered, "Blue Lady, Roger, you really think we can make this stand?" She swept the crowd with her gaze. "Does it even matter who you are unless we think we can beat that army? Look at us!"

"Of course it matters," Chaussen said. "We need to know if he's gotten us into this by lies alone."

Caterina's worry gave way to indignation, to the moment they both had always known must come. "I am your Defender of the Weak, Roger—how best am I to save them? If we continue to support you, we'll die."

Roger stood caught by those pleading stares and the crown that pinned him and knew that, unless he would allow them to kill each other, moment had come to break their hearts.

Chapter

———

Eight

Honest and True

Tears streamed as Caterina faced him down, grim and grown, bitter and afraid. "Honest and true, Roger, are you the son of King Agravaine?"

"No." His voice broke.

"Louder—say it again—are you the son of a king? Have you any royal blood at all?"

He lifted his head and saw the hundred who surrounded them. In the front row, Gwillim and the butcher, clinging together.

He swallowed and found his voice. "I am none. I have none. Everything you think of me, all that I've told you, is a lie. Honest and true. I've been lying to all of you for weeks. This entire battle, this war, the dead and the wounded—it's all born of my lies."

"But why?" Conor said. "For the power? For the wealth? What ever made you do it?"

"He did it for his mother," Caterina replied.

"And for yours," Roger met Conor's eye, "though I did not know it then."

He wet his lips. "It didn't begin with my mother's imprisonment; it began years earlier with every execution, degradation and humiliation. If anything, her arrest was the spur to end it." He scuffed the heel of the boot he'd once licked. "I misspoke earlier, my lord. I have not always spoken lies. I told you it didn't matter when you chose to fight evil, so long as you make the right choice. This—" he touched the crown, then lifted it down—"tearing down the tyrant was the right choice. And yes I lied to make it so." He held out the crown, low, and Caterina took it from his hand. He let his blade fall, and stood there, armored and naked before them.

"How will you be served under his brother? You heard his threat—that's the kind of king he'll be. Stand with me, fight with me. Together, we can do this; we've done it before."

"Or we get slaughtered in the trying," Chaussen said. "How many are still willing to die for you?"

"It isn't for me! It never has been." Roger's fists clenched as if he could hold on to them all. "It's for the kingdom we all deserve, lord and peasant. For the kingdom we earned."

"You'd rather we bargain with our lives, not your own. If you loved us as much as you claim, wouldn't you be the first to make the sacrifice?"

The Hearth Witch's Son

"And condemn you all to be what you were or worse?"

The butcher said, "At least we'd have a chance at living."

Roger's lips parted, but he had no rejoinder.

Gwillim met his eye for a moment, and the boy's lips trembled, then he buried his face in the butcher's bloody apron. The man shifted his great cleaver to hold the boy tighter and shield the child's eyes from Roger's disgrace. The silence in the yard was complete. Some of his army stood with tears upon their cheeks, and some with rising fury, faces twisted and livid as if his betrayal scalded them all. Hissing began, a pot close to the boiling point

"Let us finish what must be done," Caterina said, her voice cracking. "All we need do is denounce him, and the rest of us can live. I don't want my old life back any more than the rest of you, but at least I'll have a life to return to." She lifted the crown in her hand. "Let us give the crown to the man who should be king."

If only he could believe his life would ransom all of theirs. Roger's folly led them to this, to a state even worse than what they had left.

A chorus of cries greeted Caterina's gesture. Her eyes glinted, though whether in sorrow or in fear he could not be sure. Fists raised in the air, swords and spears and kitchen knives, shears and axes and pitchforks. As they had gathered here, ready to fight, every person's presence gave him strength, and now they took it back again, leaving him shaken. Roger tried to wet his lips, but his mouth had gone dry. All of his words evaporated, his voice withered to nothing.

"We cannot trust the duke to preserve our lives, or our freedom," Conor said. "Remember what Agravaine did to traitors," but his voice sounded feeble in the rising clamor.

"That's why we must claim it," Chaussen answered. "This is our chance to show our fealty. The kitchen boy led us astray; he led us into this, we can still atone."

"Let's take his head and have done," another voice echoed, and the crowd surged forward, pushing toward the mound of rubble.

"Let me through," called a voice in the distance as the crowd pressed closer.

"Conor's right—you can't—" Roger started to say, and the man nearest cuffed his face.

"Shut up, boy, you've done enough damage. We don't have to listen to your lies."

"Then listen to Lord Conor! Find the Lady Rania—"

The man hit him again, hard enough to blur his vision.

Chaussen plucked the ever-present kerchief from Caterina's sleeve and grabbed Roger's chin, shoving the kerchief into his mouth where he choked on it. A former groom used to wrangling tougher beasts than him unbuckled the gorget, leaving his neck exposed, and stripped the mail shirt.

Roger kicked off the groom and landed a solid punch on one of the knights, with some wild plan of escaping to the gorge. He got half a step before a foot slammed into his kidney.

A half dozen others joined in the fight, pummeling him

down, ready to take his head and have some hope of living another day. Ribs cracked and he couldn't breathe around the gag.

The groom wrenched Roger's arms together at his back and bound them with his leather belt. "You, with the knife!" He pointed toward the crowd.

"Seems fitting it's me," the butcher said. He gently set off Gwillim. The butcher lumbered up the slope and grabbed one of Roger's elbows, the groom taking the other. They hauled him up the rubble mound to where a stone trough lay. A few knights and laundresses, seeing the path of his captors, clambered up and turned up the trough, grunting with the effort, they leveled it as best they could, readying it for his blood.

The groom shoved him to his knees, rocks gouging into him. With the broad, blunt end of his chopping blade, the butcher pushed Roger's head down. His throat slammed against the stone and he choked at the pressure.

"Hold, good people, I pray you, hold." Rania's voice.

Roger sobbed without sound, without tears, his throat scraping the stone. The smell of the butcher's bloody blade hovered in the air near his head.

"The duke has given us a night, my friends, I pray you we must use it." Her voice drew closer, her footsteps stalking the rubble, and others shifted with her. "Of course you're furious—we all are, but we must be cautious and we must not give up all that we have gained. You fear the knights outside, as well you should—I fear them, too. But our too-hasty surrender plays into their hands. They have planned for this as we have not. They offer us the night, and we should take it, we must make ourselves ready. We must talk of our demands. If we give up the usurper and all of our gains, we need some guarantees in return."

The rumbling that had greeted her opening turned speculative.

"What does her grace Caterina say?" called one voice from below.

"Yes—what say you, Caterina?"

For a moment, nobody spoke, and Roger wished he could see her face, her transformation from a scullion to a leader—if any of them survived the night to carry it forward. At last, Caterina sighed. "You know the gentry, my lady, especially this duke, better than any of us. You're right. Yes, I agree."

"What about him?" The flat of the butcher's blade thwacked Roger's head, driving the stone lip harder against him.

"Hold him until morning," Rania said. "We offer our list of demands and get some surety from the duke, only then do we execute him as our assurance and toss down his head."

Her flippant tone ached. Was she just prolonging her own chance to once more escape the duke? At least each of them would have another night, a few more hours to live for him, a few more hours of freedom for her. The blade lifted from his head. "Fair enough," said the butcher, "but the dungeon's broke."

"I'll take him to the mews. It's central and secure, no gaps in the walls."

"Right. Need some volunteers to guard the prisoner!"

A strong hand bunched the back of his jerkin and peeled him up. He nearly pitched forward off the mound, struggling for breath around the gag, pain gripping his ribcage and stomach from his beating. Rania pulled him steady with an arm about his chest. Her hand lay flat against his thundering heart, their faces brought cheek to cheek. Her sword rested just under his chin and across his shoulder. The blade nicked his bruised throat with every ragged breath as she held him. "Let's go."

More than once, her strength kept him upright as he stumbled, dazed with pain. The crowd bunched up before them. Lords sneering, laborers spitting in his face. She kept him on, half-supporting, half hauling until they reached the low brick mews with its snuggly fitted doors and narrow grated windows. The butcher pulled back the bolts on the outside of the first door, only the lower part. Rania shifted her grip to let him down. He braced for another impact on his bruised knees, but she softened the fall, keeping his weight, sinking down with him, until she could push his head under the half-height door. Her hand lingered on his hair. For a moment again, her lips drew close to his cheek and she breathed, "You were a fine king, Roger. I wish the tale did not end like this."

Then the groom's boot kicked him inside, sprawling into the stifling shit and feathered muck of the falcon's close.

CHAPTER

NINE

Taking Flight

ROGER SCRAMBLED TO HIS KNEES, dragging his face up from the foul flooring. With a screech and a rush of wings, a falcon plunged toward his scalp. He gave a strangled cry, ducking, and scraped his face against the wall. Laughter echoed outside his prison. A falcon was the symbol of the Blue Lady, and its attack scoured the last of his hopes.

His breath came in lumps, hard as undercooked beef. He coughed and gagged, finally dislodging the kerchief from his mouth to breathe more deeply. The very act of breathing tore at his throat and the thick air of the mews smothered him. Dodging a low perch, he shuffled on his knees back toward the door, and sank into the corner as the falcon plunged again, screaming with Caterina's voice, with the voice of every scullion whose trust he fouled. Just like some lying member of the gentry, as Caterina said weeks ago on the tower when she first spoke of killing him. Blue Lady's love, she should've done it then and had it over. A fine king said Rania? A little lie of comfort for a man who waited death at dawn.

He crouched in the gloom as the last sun vanished. At least the darkness soothed the falcon so she no longer tore at him in her fury. In the darkness, he made himself small, curled into an egg, and yet, for the first time in months, able to breathe again. In the darkness, he could be naked, stripped of all pretension, stripped of the guises the crown urged upon him. In the darkness, he imagine his own eyes reflected, glittering, vacant as if the moon had been taken from the sky, and he thought of the Blue Lady's fall, tossed down by the Lords, somewhere between the heavens and the sea—had she ever lifted her arms and tried to fly?

With no pillow but the brick, and no mattress but the accumulated feathers and fouling of the other occupant, Roger slept fitfully. He startled awake with the sensation of the falcon's talons along his shoulder and the slumped back of his head. It was not attacking now, but what? Exploring? Kneading him, and sometimes brushing its beak against him. "Hullo?" he croaked.

At his movement, the falcon hesitated, then resumed its grooming and finally settled again into the crook of his shoulder at the back of his neck, a hot, soft presence like a heart that beat outside his body. Like him, it just wanted a more comfortable place to roost.

"My lord king," a whisper at the grated door.

"Conor?" He managed, though his throat felt parched and rusty. He straightened his head, and the falcon ruffled, snicked its beak and settled again.

"Your Majesty, forgive me not coming sooner. We spoke late into the night about what to do, it's only now I've taken on guarding you."

To keep him company until dawn? "And have you decided?"

He caught a sudden whiff of slick, sweet olive oil and frowned into the darkness. No, not so dark any more. The dawn approached. Had Conor been sent to bring him up to the block? His muscles trembled and he wished again for darkness.

The door opened softly, on freshly oiled hinges, and Conor's hand groped, then found Roger's head. "Stay quiet, my lord king. Peace. There's many guards about though most of them are sleeping." He guided Roger outside with an arm at his shoulders, the other to protect his head from smacking the low door. He kept Roger's arm as they rose together, Roger feeling shaky. The falcon swept out its wings and flew upward in a broad circle only to land upon the roof of the mews they had just escaped.

"Always the right time to fight evil, Your Majesty, isn't it?" The barest edge of dawn showed Conor's face pale and resolved, his eyes glinting. "But it should've been sooner." His supportive hands slid down to Roger's bound wrists, working roughly, then the belt tumbled free and Roger brought his hands around, his fingers fat as sausages and tingling.

"I am in your debt, my lord. I can't ever thank you enough." He rubbed his hands and wrists.

"Patrols at the west side are low, near the gorge. There's a narrow path down—can you climb?" Conor steered him in that direction, stepping past a pair of men who slept curled together under a cloak. "The Lady Rania has vanished. I think she likely went that way."

Roger's heart sank at first—he had imagined she, the first among the gentry to join him, would also be the last to leave—but perhaps her departure meant that she would live instead of dying or being seized by her brutal betrothed. He imagined her riding the hills, dressed in black, an outlaw and a bandit and a beauty still unravished. "Gods speed her to safety," he whispered.

"I can't blame her leaving," Conor said. "Given what's likely to be her fate, no matter how the dawn breaks. In any case, I think you can get out that same way."

"I could," Roger said. He'd taken the path from time to time in search of cliff swallow nests to yield eggs for Agravaine's plate when ordinary chicken eggs just wouldn't do. He glanced around the quiet castle yard, the towers outlined above in starlight, and down low by the rosy hints of dawn. In the yard toward the gate, most of his army slept in huddled mounds or gathered round small fires, the thick cloaks of barons spread from their shoulders to those of their companions, people they would, last year, have slapped for touching their clothes. "I could escape that way, but I won't."

Conor clutched his shoulder. "My lord king—"

He shook his head. "You know better."

"I know only that you won the crown and are more worthy to wear it than any man I've ever known. You need to

103

go, or hide until the gates open. They'll search, but I'm sure you know places."

"You're not leaving, are you? Or hiding from the fight? There's at least one more thing to try. So long as that is true, I cannot leave, and I will not hide."

Conor's brows drew together, his eyes threatening a storm of tears. "I gave you your freedom, Your Majesty, I thought you would use it."

"And so I shall. For courage, and not for cowardice." He gripped Conor's shoulder. "Caterina and the others, they're not wrong. I got us all into this. One way and another I will be here until the end."

"It should not come at the hands of your friends."

"At least they might be merciful about it—I think the duke will not."

"You have another plan, though?"

"A notion. If I cannot call upon my father's lineage to save, me, perhaps my mother's will do. Go back, Conor—be as surprised as anyone to learn of my escape."

Conor gripped his arm in turn and released him. "You are nothing, Your Majesty, if not surprising." He gave a slight bow and slipped away into the rising dawn.

The falcon preened on its roof-top, one leg stretched out, swiping its beak first one way, then the other, as if it were sharpening its talons. It ruffled its feathers and settled in. Come dawn, it would strike the first thing it saw with feathers —or come to the first man who offered meat.

The Hearth Witch's Son

Roger stripped off the king's boots—they were too large in any case—and hurried on swift and silent feet down to the arched kitchen door. Never empty during his tenure there, this day, it was. The remains of their preparations lay tumbled about, except where the loaves had been taken to eat or the pantries opened to feed everyone sheltering in the yard tonight. His army had gathered in from the fields and villages as the duke approached, rushing before the trumpet's blare, but someone had regulated their stomachs, or the whole kitchen would be ransacked. He lay odds on Caterina, a familiar face with new powers. She had grown, for good or ill; enough that she could now lead the accusations against him, his Defender of the Weak—even from him, as once she swore. He hugged himself, sliding his tingling hands into his armpits, like a child cast again into the moors with only his mother to guide him. Every muscle ached, but he would not fall.

"Rog? That you?" She shuffled up the narrow stair from her little chamber. "'Tis you, boy, but you do reek, don't you?" She slapped away the feathers and straw and bits of bone stuck to him from the falcon's supper. "How'd ye get—never mind, boy, come along." She tugged at his arm, but he resisted.

"I've come to ask your help, Mother. Against the duke's army."

"Cor!" she chuckled at that and slapped his arm this time in jest. "What can I do, old woman that I am? All I do's pluck herbs and sweep ashes."

"Help us now, Mum—with whatever skill you can. We

105

need you." He gripped her hands in his, though his fingers still felt chubby from his restraints.

"What skill, boy? Ye know what I can do: take the hurt from a wound, alright. What else? Make up herbs and potions, poison the pests; take the smoke from a fire, spring the fire in the hearth. Maybe a charm for luck or a spell for grace."

"Small powers, but something. Why else did the king arrest you? A spell to make their soldiers clumsy, a charm for misfortune —a blast of smoke that stifles their horses. Even the bat poison." His throat hurt where the trough had squeezed him, his scalp from the cuts of the falcon's beak, his stomach and ribs from the beating. He would dearly love to just lie down and rest, but he could not, not with an army at his door.

"Blue Lady, Roger; I can't believe ye still think ye can win! I've got skill enough to cover our escape, just you and I. Come away with me and live."

And abandon Gwillim, Conor, Rania, all the people who counted on him, the people he had encouraged to come this far. "You're my own mother—can't you believe with me? Just a little longer."

"Ay, Roger." Her head was shaking, her dark tangle of hair twitching against her shoulders, and she would not meet his eye. "Something ye should know, Rog, before you say so." Her lips hung slack for a moment, then she swallowed and seemed to find a little strength. "Not only are ye no king's bastard, Rog, you're not even mine." She gave the smallest shrug.

The Hearth Witch's Son

For a moment, he thought pain and fear had gotten the better of him and he had misunderstood her. He shook off his shock. "Not…not yours? Not your son?"

"Twas during my wanderings, finding a spot here and there, helping out at a village, like that. Your mum was a carter's wife with four others at home. Little before the Demon War, round about the time of the orc raids." She gave a shrug that carried a sigh. "Ye were sickly-like, nowt I couldn't cure, I thought. But yer mum'd had enough of you. Cried all the time, you did, the first couple years—always did have that powerful voice, even as a tyke, and she'd had enough. Her man'd been taken up by the king's conscription, fighting off the orcs. She asked a poison of me, or asked, would it better to smother you, to have done with you gently. Ye looked scrawny enough, but I thought to see would ye live or no, and so I took you up. Witches don't have children, do they? What with the whole countryside getting up in arms—and I mean that, honest and true—a child'd make me look like just another refugee. Harmless old kitchen drudge, me, and my husband lost to the orcs, same as anyone."

Roger's knees went weak, and he sank to the floor, too numb to stop himself falling. No royal bastard. Not even the hearth witch's son, but just somebody's unwanted whelp, an excess child, and an old woman in need of proof against witch-craft. Her voice rumbled over him, as if the whole of the castle broke into stones and tumbled down upon his bowed head.

"You're nothing, Rog. Nothing but a charming, lying, little sneak of a boy."

CHAPTER

TEN

All in the Telling

SHE WAITED A MOMENT, as if expecting some reply, then went on, "Can't blame you, I guess, what you turned out to be, growing up like that. Loved you best I could, didn't I? But even I couldn't get too close "til all your sores was mended and ye stopped yer bawling. What's a boy to do but find his own way? And that voice. Always thought the bawling was what made ye strong in the end." She bobbed her head. "Almost like witch-craft, innit, the way folk listen to you?"

She tousled his hair, patted his cheek, and said, "So then, let's get on with it. You and me, we'll find another kitchen someplace, eh? This whole affair's nothing to do with the likes of us. Two old rotters, might's rot off by ourselves, eh? Mebbe the next place we go, we'll make out ye're a bard. Your fancy clothes aren't so bad off, aside from the blood." She looked him over, tugging his jerkin into place, ruffling the lace at his collar.

Roger's eyes slid shut, burning with tears he could not shed. His chest clenched and he could get no air. He was noth-ing but the lies she told him and the greater ones he spun out for himself, like a crafty little spider, good for keeping the flies down, otherwise unwanted. Honest and true.

The burning at his eyes consumed him. It swelled through his skull as if he could shoot flames out of his eyes, as if his very hair would catch fire and he roared to his feet. "Why are telling me this—any of this? Blue Lady, Mother, have I not been low enough? Have I not been shackled in the bird shit all night long that you have to come and shit on me yourself?"

"I've been with you from the start, Roger, and you've not been listening. You're no king, you're no witch's blood, you're only yerself. I thought, if ye knew, ye'd give up all this and get on back to where we belong." She flapped a hand at the kitchen and castle beyond. "I want ye t' live, Roger. Can't ye see that?"

His fist drummed at his hollow chest where any sense of human connection should be, the void he scrambled to fill for all of his life, and now he finally knew where it came from, who had dug that pit and pitched him in it. Vegetables on the table rocked as he slammed his fists into it, his hands aching. He grabbed an onion and flung it into the fireplace where it cracked against the spit and set it turning of its own accord, roasting him in his fury. His breath burned, his shoulders quaking.

She shrank before him. "I've never seen ye like this, Rog. It's not you, it isn't."

"How can I even tell what is me? It's one thing to know I've lied myself a crown, another to find my whole life has been nothing but lies." He swallowed hard, his throat seared. "You know they're going to kill me, Mum, one side or the other. My friends will or my enemies." He took a deep breath, staring down at her, finally understanding why they bore no resemblance in form or face or nature. "Why couldn't you just stay quiet and let me take it to my grave?"

Her lips bent, the characteristic droop at their corners sinking even lower, and she sighed. "How was I to tell you before now? Never made no claims about yer father, did I? But you always had a notion when I wouldn't say—making me a princess disgraced by her true love, a witch who seduced a knight, a woman mourning a man who died to save her, even an acolyte abused by the Lords' monks when you were old enough to know such things. Ah, Roger. All those tales ye made of me, making me greater than I was, braver and brighter and better—why'd I give up all of that for the truth? For you being angry, finding your mum chucked ye from her bosom. I've been a mum to you, haven't I?" She nodded to herself, suddenly fragile before his anger.

What little they had, they had always shared. She told him stories when he was small, a way to fill the cold hours before dawn, to fill a mind when you could not fill a stomach, and as he grew, he had returned that kindness. His tales were always more grand than hers, until he topped them off with the greatest lie of his life, and fought and won a war in her name.

She gave a little chuckle. "Y'know, Rog, 'tis the first time ye've made a story with yerself the hero, innit?"

His anger churned within. What a hero he had turned

out to be, Roger Silvertongue, Betrayer of Dreams, leaving his people ever so much worse off than they'd been. His friends from the kitchen to be punished for their uprising, his friends from the gentry to be executed for treason. A handful of prisoners freed from the dungeon might claim his rule as a victory.

From the direction of the castle gate, a trumpet echoed, and Roger's head jerked up. In the doorway opposite, a shadow flickered, a form with a warrior's skirt and a blade of steel.

Of course. How else should his humiliation be complete? "Have you come to kill me?"

Rania stepped from the corridor, the sword's tip nearly brushing the ground. Her lips compressed, her eyes gleaming. "Oh, Roger."

How long had she been standing outside? No need to ask—her pity said it all.

His mother tugged at his arm. "Come, come! Our time's passing. We've got to move." Her glance darted toward the lady, back to him. He allowed himself to be drawn up. "I can cover our leaving—I've got skill enough for that."

He could leave with her and go into hiding, waiting the day that someone recognized and slew him, or maybe just living once more in the dirt, telling no more stories, knowing how many he had left behind to suffer for his lie. "Not skill enough to help us win."

"What's this 'us,' Roger? You 'n me've always been outside, haven't we? Suspected by the peasants, disdained by the swells.

Ye think ye've brought them all together." She blew out a breath of disbelief. "There's never been an 'us' in Corsevale but what you made, what you lied into being."

If only he could do it one more time. One more tale. Change the ending, but not for him. His end would be in blood. Going to his mother had been his last hope for victory, and it had brought him only a greater defeat. She had left him with nothing but his voice.

She did love him, in her way. She loved him enough to want him to go on living. She tugged on him, and he wondered how she planned to get him out of a castle full of enemies. What witchcraft might she conjure? He would betray his people one last time, leaving them without even his corpse to buy their deliverance. He had nothing left for them, no gifts save the powerful voice he had used to betray them. Almost witchcraft, his mother had called it.

He drew down a breath full of bread and blood and spices and lifted his head. She, herself had given him the answer.

He took his arm from her grasp and stepped away. "Unhand me, Mother, for I am the king."

She gawked at him, her eyes brimming and her mouth open in a tiny "o' as if she would cry out to him. Her gnarled hands, emptied, wrung together.

Roger turned away, his steps grown fleet. His heart and mind raced. He rifled the shelves and snatched a few things, filling his fists. Two strides toward the door, then Rania barred the way, Rania and her sword.

"I thought you had left," he said.

"I went to the muster point, to see if we had more allies."

He blinked and nearly smiled. Of course she hadn't run, not even from the fate that awaited her in the duke's hands. "And have we?"

She shook her head, shrugged. "Nearly a hundred, but like the people within the wall, eager and unskilled. I told them I would signal for their attack. They don't know—I didn't tell them, about you. I thought of staying to lead them but I needed to know what happened here, if you were—"she broke off, her expression bleak. "Instead, I found you'd escaped," she breathed. "The others on the council think you gone already, betraying them again. I thought I might know better." Her gaze flicked over his face. "What now?"

"Go to the attic, my lady," he told her. "Those bat bombs, there's dozens of them. Rat poison in the pantries as well. If you rally a brigade and pitch them down among the horses, we can sicken some of our attackers and sow confusion for a counter attack. The gates won't hold against a siege, and neither will our resources. Tell the army to cover their mouths and noses and muster a sally against the duke. When the chaos strikes, then so do we." Another stride and she stood suddenly before him, straight as steel herself.

"They're not your army, Roger, not any more."

"You're right—they aren't, and I cannot lead them." Roger met her eye. "What choices remain? We can fight, or we can run. If we fight, we might prevail—but against three hundred armed and trained fighting men, our chances are slim. If we run, we'll be hunted, haunted by what we could have been." His mother shrank beneath his look. "If you—kill me. If we surrender. What then? He strings up my council and any other leaders. His soldiers ravish the land while he ravishes you. He becomes Agravaine all over again and worse."

Her face paled, and she did not deny it. "You want me to lead them—assuming they'll fight. What will you be doing?"

"Coming with me," his mother pleaded somewhere at his back.

He shook his head, a denial that cast off cobwebs and kitchen muck and the last of the falcon's down as if he were ready, at last, to take flight. "If our army won't fight and they can't surrender, they'll need an escape path, and I'm the only one who can make it." He traced her features, captured by the moist green of her eyes, the determined set of her lips. "What will I be doing? The only thing I'm good for. I'll be lying."

Roger turned away and swept past her. She tipped her sword from his path and let him go.

CHAPTER

—— ⁓ ——

ELEVEN

The Greatest Lie

ROGER STRODE UP THE STEPS from the kitchen, moving fast, praying to the Blue Lady to defend him a little longer. In the yard, people gathered in knots, their voices shrill and frightened, or low and resigned. People staggered to their feet, roused as he had been by the trumpet's blast. The barest pale light of day spread over the scene, but most of it remained in shadows, furtive, gray and dismal. The mound of rubble rose ahead of him, almost an inner wall. In its lee, a few people huddled around a fire: Caterina and Chaussen sharing a cloak, the butcher, Gwillim, the groom, a pair of knights. Atop the mound, a single figure, still arrayed for battle, kneeling unmistakably in prayer.

Roger swept his gaze over the crowd. "Your Grace Caterina of Fesburg, where is my crown?"

They startled, the knights immediately drawing against him. As his voice echoed across the yard, his people scrambled to attention, found their weapons, began to form their lines as they had the night before. The falcon launched from her mews and soared upward, carrying his spirit with her. In the faces of his people today, he saw wonder, suspicion, surprise. Always surprising, Conor had said. Roger grinned and offered a slight bow with a pivot to take them all in.

"Duchess, my crown."

"Seize him now! Now!" Chaussen ordered. The butcher jumped up, cleaver in hand.

"You're still here," Caterina blurted, "When you weren't there, we assumed—"

"At the very least, we knew we had a traitor among us," Chaussen said, glaring toward the man who prayed.

Roger closed the distance between them, but kept his hands low to the sides, circling a little to keep the armed knights before him. He dropped his voice, not wanting to be heard beyond the walls. "I am the man who killed the king. I am the man who raised this army, and you expected me to run from the fight? Even if the fight must be with you? Liar I may be, but coward I am none."

"But the duke—" Chaussen began.

"Has asked for my head, and I shall bring it to him. But he'll have to take it himself from the top of the gate."

Caterina spun about, searching, and the two body servants stretched and shrugged into the day. "Where is the crown? Where's it gone?"

"Well, you're not going to give it to him," Chaussen said. "You know what we discussed. The list of demands, the guarantees—"

Outside, the trumpet blew again, and the herald's voice called out, "His Grace, Mariux Duke of Denneton demands his

117

price. Throw down the head of the usurper, and you shall meet with justice."

Roger's belly clenched, but he said, "He needs to see me."

"Allow me," Conor said. He descended from where he had been praying and stood tall at Roger's back. His long shadow revealed him, sword in one hand, shield in the other. He flicked a glance at Roger, who gave a cautious nod. "We'll display him on the tower, so the duke knows we're ready to bargain."

"Good, yes," Caterina said. "We'll bring up the list."

"No, Your Grace, don't expose yourselves yet," Conor warned. "Come then, kitchen boy."

Roger retreated before him, letting it seem he was driven at the point of Conor's blade. Still his man? Blue Lady, let it be so—let the long night not have eroded Conor's spirit as it had the others. Caterina and Chaussen and the rest watched him go, already whispering, a scroll brought out. Toward the back of the yard where the workshops edged the walls and the castle stood, a different wave passed, Rania moving among those who had retreated from what would happen at the gates, retreating from their fate. Roger marched resolutely toward his own. As he entered the cool of the tower, Conor stepped with him, closing the distance between them, his sword lowered. "Your Majesty, I am half sick for this."

Roger paused on the landing and pivoted to face him, standing two steps below. "Conor. Stay here. There's no need for you to see."

The Hearth Witch's Son

"Are you just—offering yourself for their archers?"

"I am getting you all a way out. When it comes, take it."

"What're you going to do?"

Roger shook his head. "Better if I surprise all of you, on both sides."

"You may need this." Conor sheathed his sword, and switched his shield, revealing the crown looped over his left arm. He glanced at Roger's fisted hands, frowned, and placed the crown upon his head. "Fare you well, Your Majesty." He took a moment to level the crown, then he squeezed Roger's shoulder, and let him go.

The stairs dwindled before him and when Roger stepped up to the platform, it was as if he pulled himself free of a sucking darkness. Dawn stroked down his hair and warmed his face. The sky above him shimmered blue, spotted with clouds, and the falcon soared like the Blue Lady's blessing on his doom, or on the way he chose to face it. The duke's army stood in their gleaming ranks, the herald about to call out for a second time. A thick log lay in the first ranks of footmen, waiting to break down his gate.

Atop the gate tower, his three soldiers jostled, one pulling a dagger, but Roger said, "Put that up, Man, or save it for the enemy. Take shelter, all of you."

At the sound of his voice, one of the crossbowmen pointed and the focus of the gathered army shifted from the gate, to the tower. The duke turned his horse, "Usurper! How dare you—"

"Your Grace." Roger spread his arms. His mistake yesterday had been allowing his enemy to speak too much. "You ask me that when you dare assail me in my own keep. You discard the tale of my birth, so be it. You say I am no king, for my father was none. So be it. My mother, sir, is another matter. She is a witch, and one of the last."

The duke's horse stamped at the sudden tension of its reins.

"What is he doing up there?" Caterina hissed somewhere behind him. "Get him down! He'll get us all killed!"

"No," Conor's voice. "No, Your Grace, listen—I beg of you, listen."

Roger pitched his voice to be heard, to carry across walls and fields and roads. A thousand tales he told before, including the one that brought him here. The greatest lie he'd ever told. Or so he thought, until today. "And if my blood carries no hint of royalty, it carries still the taint of magic. Honest and true, my lords, I tell you so. How else was I to rule here? How else does a kitchen boy kill a king? How does he raise up an army of both peasants and lords? How does he win the hearts of so many, when he has nothing—" his voice caught on the word—"is nothing worthy of their attention. With magic, I tell you! By spells and by sorcery I have held them. With spells have I made my weapons and by magic, forged my army." He raised one fist to the sky.

"For I control the freedom of the air, and I can conjure the birds to my hand." The hungry falcon screamed then plunged, its sharp wings folded. Roger stifled his wince as its talons wrapped his fingers, its head bobbing and rubbing his fist as if in obeisance as it tried to get at the meat he had hidden within.

"So, too, I control the freedom of your minds. All of you will be mine." He stretched out his other hand, aiming his finger at them, turning a slow circle to meet the eyes of as many as he could, and all the while letting a stream of fine powder trickle into the air. "I conjure your youth, the dreams you had of greatness. I cast you back to some far away kitchen or feasting hall, to a time of joy and prosperity. I conjure you by those delights, and I say to you that if you lay down your arms, I will make you one of us."

The wind carried the powder, a handful of cinnamon. Men's eyes widened as the scent reached them with a tingle and a memory. Apples baked hot, a roast made rich, a longing for better things.

The horses stomped, reared, and tossed their manes, retreating from him, from the sharp dust that swirled toward their faces. The lead knights fought their mounts, wheeling about. In the second rank, the crossbowmen waited, some with their eyes watering—from the effect of the spice, or of their own memories? Some of them readied their weapons, bolts to the brace. Only one thing he needed, the only thing he had ever needed: for them to believe in him.

"And if I can raise an army and force them to my will with magic, what, Your Grace, might I do with you?" He aimed his glare at the duke. Then he slowly stretched out his arm and unfurled his fingers. He chanted nonsense words in his most glorious tone. He met the duke's terrified gaze and aimed the ferocity of his empty hand.

"Shut him up and take him down!" The duke roared. "A hundred gold for the man who hits—a thousand for who brings his head!"

"Fie, Your Grace!" Roger shouted, and the falcon launched from his hand. "I shall call down upon you—"

With a screech, the falcon whipped back its wings and snatched the first bolt from the air, hoping for live prey.

Roger spun aside at the stroke of its feathers.

With the twang of string and a shock of wind, a second crossbow bolt tore across his throat. Roger gasped around the agony and drew no breath. His knees buckled and he fell. He plunged from the sky to the yard behind, as if he had been felled by the falcon's strike. He crashed hard and spoke in blood. At least, it was no lie.

CHAPTER

TWELVE

The Tale's End

ROGER LAY AS HE HAD FALLEN, curled on his side, his right arm numb from the elbow down, his throat searing as he choked on his own blood.

"Your Majesty!" A man's voice, frightened, pleading.

Stones tumbled striking his back and legs as someone hurried down the rubble behind him. A shaky hand touched his arm and withdrew as Roger jerked with the pain.

"A liar to the end," Another man, bitter. "For what? For a quick death?"

"Roger?" A woman's voice, very close, a voice he'd known for years in the kitchen. "Blue Lady."

"Why would he make up a story like that? Witchcraft? He must've known they'd kill him." The hand returned, pinning him. "Hold still, Your Majesty," a whisper, then "Dear Lords."

"Let's take his head, then. That's what they want. We'll just do it. I've still got my cleaver."

"No," Caterina said. "I can't bear it. No."

"Fine then, open the gates. Cast us on the duke's mercy, we'll see—"

"Hush," she said suddenly. "My lord Conor? You said they'd kill us anyway, at least those of us new, because we supported him?"

"I believe they will, Your Grace. I'm sorry." Conor worked over him, clamping a hand to the blood that spilled from Roger's throat, trying to staunch the flow.

"No," she said again, but stronger now. "Because he gave us the means to survive this. We're not responsible, he is. He was a witch—he just told them all. What could a witch not do?" She gasped and let out a sob. "Ah, Blue Lady, he was trying to save us."

Listen to her, Roger wished he could say, but his voice had gone, and he did not know if it would ever return. He tried to point to her, to call attention. He gagged and strained against the hands that held him.

"She's right." Conor. "He told me on the stairs that he'd give us an escape path. Open the gates and say that we're free, released from his magic. Praise the lords, praise the duke for our deliverance, praise the wretched bowman who slew the witch who enslaved us all." His voice cracked. He cradled Roger as he struggled for breath and coughed out his life. "Now—if we're to do it, we must act now."

"Out of the way! Get away!" Rania. No pain, not even death itself could prevent him knowing that voice. "Your Majesty. Lords, we've got to help him." She stroked the hair back from his face.

"His throat's torn open, my lady. Is it faster for him to

bleed out or to drown in his own blood? I want him to die no more than you do, but by the Lords they'll have no more from him." Conor's voice, near breaking. "They know they hit him. If we're to pretend his magic is over, we have to act."

"You were on the tower with us, Duchess Rania," Caterina said, very low. "When Agravaine was killed. You know what he wanted."

"You're ready to ruin what he really wants—what he wants is for us to live. For the kingdom he believed in to go on, even without him." Rania's strong hands took over from Conor to press a wadded cloth to his wound.

"He freed us from the king, and now he's bound us to a lie, to claim we had no part in the battles we won." Caterina. He could see her now, through a single tear-blurred eye that had a hard time staying open. "And for what—for enslavement at the hands of another? Will the duke even accept our demands, no matter what we give him? I have tasted freedom, lord, I'd rather die."

"Cor—you're not serious." The butcher—what was his name? What did it matter.

"Shut up, all of you. Fight if you're going to fight—I've spread his plans, use his mother's potions—go!" Rania cried. "For Lords' love, don't plague him with your indecision." Roger wished he could cheer her on, but he only shuddered. Feeling returned to his fingers, and it was fire. Please, yes, please, just leave him die.

"He told me in the kitchen," Conor said, "it doesn't

matter when you choose to fight evil, what matters is, you make the right choice."

"We weren't under no spell when we won the castle, my lord. He told his greatest lie so that we could live," the butcher said. "You'd fight against it? Against three hundred men?"

Caterina said, "His greatest lie was the kingdom he thought could be. That's what we fight for."

"Yes, Your Grace, we do," Conor answered. "You go for the tower, the potions, and I'll rally the army." And, in a tumble of stones, they were gone.

Rania swept the green sash from her hair and wound it about his throat, trying to save him. Every brush of her fingers against him sent a shock of pain. He tremored in her arms. Would she hold him now, waiting for the moment they could take off his head? Rather let him die on the field of battle, at the gates of his victory.

"Let me go," he whispered. "I'm not afraid to die." His voice faded, dwindling in a ribbon of blood and of pain. He had no words, no voice. He produced only a strangled groan. His lying voice silenced, every breath sliced at him as if the bolt had been a hatchet, and his throat no more than firewood.

She shifted her grip, bringing him closer against her chest, her hand rising to cradle his face and her eyes shone like the green and distant hills. "If I must fight off every person of your own army and his, my king, they will not have you."

"Rania. I love you." He swallowed and coughed the taste of blood. He ratcheted another breath, and told her,

"Honest and true." His throat buzzed as he tried to speak and it stung like a thousand bees. She stared, as if trying to find the meaning in the blood, but those last words she must seen a hundred times upon his lips.

"Oh, Roger." Rania shook her head, her hair tumbling loose around her shoulders, screening their faces in a fall of silken comfort like the curtains of the king's own bed. "Honest you have never been, my king, but always true."

He shivered. Her image blurred and swam like the heat of a rising summer, or the mist on the fish ponds in the morn-ing. Rania bent nearer still, and he wished he could turn away. Let his blood be spilled upon the ground, neither witch, nor royal, don't let it stain her hands. She drew his arm up over her shoulders, tucked her other arm under his knees and dragged him to her chest, staggering up.

A rush of wind, a cry of voices, a clash of arms—or only the rolling waves within his skull, the clash of darkness, the longing for light. She carried him, stumbling and weaving, until her hands were not alone. Three, four, how many it took to bear him, he did not know.

"Here, the kitchen!"

"Clear that table—get the surgeon, go!"

The clatter now of pots and the heat of the hearth, the smells of blood and bone and beef and turnips. Had Conor's filleting been all for naught? It did not scent the air. No, that had been days ago. They lay him on the work table, his head toward the side, his blood now dribbling to the floor. They made him a pillow of a flat round loaf, and blankets of linen when his shivering grew. They tucked warm stones around him like a roast to be cooked all day long.

Rania sank to her knees before him. His blood on her skirts for certain now. She clasped his hand in her own.

"Where's his mother?" somebody demanded, and Rania's grip tightened, nearly hot enough now to keep his shaking at bay.

"She's gone," Rania snapped, "she—"

"Here I am, Rog. Right here. Making some things for our friends at the gate."

Rania looked up, tearing her eyes from him. "Magic?"

"What I've got. 'Tisn't much. But my son's made a kingdom from nothing. He asked for my help, seems I'll offer what I can." His mother's gnarled fingers kneaded his scalp and settled at the back of his neck. Tingling warmth rushed through him, washing away the pain, if not the terrible choking as he drowned in his own blood. He would take any comfort, no matter how small. Gratitude flooded him, knowing she had not gone.

"Stand back, please, ladies. I need room to work." A brusque voice. The surgeon.

"Be gentle with him, doctor. You've no idea how deeply he's wounded."

"I will, my lady."

"Come then, Mother, and we'll do what we can." Rania clung a moment longer to his hand, then ducked low, her voice falling to a whisper at his ear. "This day might see us dead, Roger Silvertongue. Lords willing, we both shall live, and either way, my king, I'll come to you. If I have not misjudged your heart."

Had she ever? As he parted his lips to answer and knew he couldn't, tears spilled over, and she stroked them away. "Shh, shh. If ever you had spoken your love to me, I would have called you liar. You have stood by me in silence, but your eyes have sung me poetry." She stroked her thumb over his lips, wiping away the blood. She kissed him—then she was gone.

CHAPTER

⁓

THIRTEEN

And Ever After?

HE SLEPT AND WOKE AND HURT AND WEPT. At first the sounds of battle reached him and he mistook them for the kitchen's clash until someone screamed and died. Shadows came and went around him. He woke again in a room that echoed with groans, and sobs, and some of them were not his own. He lay on his left side, his right arm bound up in a sling. A mattress cushioned the table where he lay, and a pillow beneath his head. From the corner of his eye he saw the gleam of metal, flickering with firelight, a ring of spearpoints gilded and bejeweled. The crown. What was it still doing there? Beyond that, down from the table where he lay, ranks of makeshift beds and restive people. A hospital with an inlaid floor. The castle's great hall stretching down toward the grand doors. Stained glass windows between the buttresses cast a rainbow gleam on the floor. At least a day or two had passed. His arm throbbed, his throat flushed with heat at every breath, but it no longer pierced him with agony.

"Are you awake, Roger?" a soft, young voice, then Gwillim's face entered his view, capped by a winding of bandage, slightly stained. "I'm to give you water. Don't move your head, but look, Cat—that is—her grace says to show your hand for yes, your fist for no. Right?"

Clever Caterina. Roger shifted the blankets over him and let his left hand show, flat.

Gwillim grinned and laughed. "You're alive, Roger—you're here. Look at us, Roger—we're still here! The castle's ours! Yours, I mean." Tears streamed from his eyes. "Right—do you want some water?" He laughed again. "Water boy, that's me."

Had he wanted to live? He hadn't meant to. Caterina, too, had lived, and Gwillim. And Rania? Would she come to him?

Water sounded beautiful just then. Roger answered with his hand, and Gwillim returned with a thin-rimmed bowl. He cradled Roger's head, lifting him a little to sip from the bowl. It tasted like blood, and stung as he swallowed. The water cooled his parched mouth, and as he drank again, the water grew more sweet. At last, he closed his fist, and lay back on his pillow, looking out over the wounded from—could it be his last battle?

"Surgeons'll be back soon." Gwillim settled by the leg of the table. "Will you sleep more?"

No. Roger's mind buzzed with questions—who had lived, and who had died and how had they ever won the day—and he had not the means to ask. He beat his fist gently on the table.

Gwillim's face furrowed, then he brightened. "Well, if

131

you're not sleeping, I can tell you a story."

Roger blinked back tears. Yes.

The boy tapped a finger on his teeth for a moment, then he said, "You'll want to know how it went. I'll tell you. It went very badly. I mean, at first, it went well—the duke didn't expect what we gave him, and his troops were a mess. When they tried to come up with that battering ram, we doused them with bat smoke, and the horses wouldn't approach, but then he brought up his archers, with flaming arrows, and we ran low on the bombs. And it looked like we were done for, for sure. It was then she rode out—Honest and true, Roger, the most beautiful thing. Lady Rania took the knights, anyone as could ride saving my lords Conor and Chaussen, who led the defense, and they threw open the gates."

Roger's fist clenched, a helpless protest, and Gwillim broke off. "You want me to stop? I shouldn't excite you, they said, if you woke."

No, again, no. He waved his hand, beckoning for more. She rode out to the duke herself? Lords, had she taken up his own hopeless intention to die? At least he had gone to it believing, if it worked, then so many could live.

Gwillim offered him more water, then carried on with his tale at Roger's mimed insistence. "Madness, eh? Some of us thought so, too, but when she led that party, they drove like a spear through the duke's knights, and we thought, they'd brought the battle to the duke, right? Only they fought their way out the other side. They set flames in the tents as they went and just kept riding.

"We all shut up the gates, of course, after your mum sent out a few surprises, something like a thousand thousand balls that fouled the feet of the enemy." He laughed in delight, remembering. "Might've been nutmeg, now I think of it. But half the duke's men went off after the lady, and the duke to lead them! Madness it looked like for us, but it turned out madness for them. Dunno where those soldiers went, Your Majesty, but they've never yet come back. Three days, it's been, and no sign."

Overconfident and angry, the duke had ridden off to claim his bride, and the remaining troops fell apart, no longer sure for whom they fought or why, arguing over what the witch-king said, and hadn't they all smelled the sweetness of the dream? A third of those remaining had surrendered, or so Gwillim eventually conveyed.

A door groaned open at the side of the hall, and Gwillim paused. "Your Grace?"

"The king—he's awake? You should've told me." Caterina hurried over, skirts bunched in her hands. Embroidered silks and velvets droopy with work and marked by tears. She slowed as she came into his view, then dropped into a curtsey, then simply sank to her knees. "The surgeons wanted you brought to your own chamber, but I thought you'd rather be here, among your people." She tried a smile, but it faltered. "Roger, my lord king, I know I don't deserve your forgiveness, but I hope—"

Roger put out his fist. Then he held up his hand to stop her, and she trailed into silence. Her shoulders slumped, and she wiped at her tears, then reached toward her sleeve, where the kerchief should be, and her hand clutched only the memory, then she buried her face in her hands. "I'm sorry, I'm sorry," she moaned. Roger gave Gwillim a nudge, and indicated for him to get Caterina's attention. How was he meant to talk with anyone if they wouldn't look at him?

She lifted her tear-streaked face, but truth be told, the tears washed tracks through the sweat, dirt and blood of battle's aftermath. Roger beckoned her closer, and she approached still on her knees, an awkward shuffle of hesitation. "I'm sorry I ever doubted you."

No, he told her, and she stopped. No, he said again, then reached out, and touched her tears. He stroked his knuckles lightly down her cheek. No apologies. Not until he could atone for the cost of his war.

"I am still a little angry, though, Roger. What you did, in trying to save us: you made it sound as if we had no choice in coming together behind you, no choice in fighting. I know it might have saved us, but that's what made it impossible for me to just accept what you offered. It's like you and your mother. At the start, she was the excuse for you saying what you did, but she wasn't the reason, not really." She looked very serious. "Just like you were the excuse for us doing what we should've done years ago. That's why we're still here. Why we chose to fight, just like you said on the tower—it wasn't just your story any more, it belongs to all of us." She reached over and ran her fingers along the points of the crown.

"That's why you are our king. Not because we couldn't do this without you, but because we know we wouldn't." Then she laughed. "That didn't make much sense did it? Blue Lady, I need some rest."

Yes, he answered, then pointed to himself and raised an eyebrow.

"Not you—you've been sleeping for days, you lazy rotter."

A rumble of voices approached, and Caterina wiped her eyes, rising. "My lords, he's awake."

"Gods be praised." Conor ran the rest of the way, rounding the corner of the table near Roger's feet, then stopped himself and dropped into a low bow. It did nothing to hide his grin. "My lord king." His glance flashed up. A long bruise marred his cheek and he straightened again much more carefully, wincing, his hand rising to his side. "Just bruised, Your Majesty, nothing to worry you."

Roger held out his hand. For a moment, Conor kept his distance, a vassal in obedience to his injured king, but Roger bent his face into fury, and beckoned again. Conor finally came, kneeling at the table. Roger caught his hand and pulled him close, a tide of relief rushing him, but still he could not ask the question, the part of the story Gwillim left untold. Conor ducked his head to rest lightly on Roger's shoulder. "Gods, Your Majesty, I cannot say how glad I am of this."

135

Roger kept his hand a long moment before he let him go.

From without, trumpets echoed. He jerked, and tried to look, but Conor caught his head, holding him to the pillow. "Truly, Your Majesty, the duke's not here to demand your head, there's no need to tear it off. You must be still to heal before we know if your voice will return."

The thought that it might allowed him to relax beneath Conor's firm hand.

Chaussen had come up a little behind Caterina. When he caught Roger's eye, he bowed deeply. He, too, wore his arm in a sling and walked stiffly. "I...Your Majesty. I was never so glad to be mistaken about a man's intentions and about his fate than I have been with you, but I expect forgiveness will take time, if ever you see fit to bestow it. You thought that we could win, and you were right."

A laundress ran up the aisle and Caterina went down to meet her, then returned, her eyes gleaming. "My lord king, the knights have returned from the hills."

Roger glared, and Conor withdrew his hands.

Roger signalled no. He put his hand up and touched his throat, thickly bandaged, and finished with silk. Was it green? A shade to match a lady's eyes. He traced the wrapping and his eyes ached.

Caterina touched his hand. "I don't know, Your Majesty," she breathed, very softly. "But these are her knights returning —they will know her fate."

His mother had taken all but his voice, and the duke

136

had taken that, but he might have more strengths after all. He pointed to himself, then to the door, and pulled back the blankets.

"We can bring them in to greet you," Conor offered.

Among the wounded who needed their rest? No.

"You're not serious, Your Majesty," Chaussen protested. "'Twas only three days ago we didn't even know if you'd survive that gash. You cannot be sitting court in your condition."

Conor replied, "I should think you had learned your lesson about telling the king what he cannot do."

Chaussen bowed himself a few steps back—out of the reach of Conor's long arm, even though he wore no sword.

"He'll need some clothes, slippers—and his throne, on the steps outside," Caterina directed. "The sunlight might do him good, as well as seeing his people." At Roger's sign of agreement, the servants around him hurried to do her bidding.

"And a thick cowl or collar," she called after them. "Something to prevent him turning his head."

In a moment, four people trundled past, carrying the throne and his remaining squires returned, carrying everything they thought he would need, or at least, what they thought could be managed. Conor gently helped him to sitting, supporting him through the wave of dizziness that resulted. He'd eaten nothing in three days, and drunk but little. The squires dressed him, buckling on a snug cowl meant for a jousting knight. Finally Conor took his good arm and helped him down to his feet, taking some of his weight. "You're sure about this, my lord king?"

A flat, emphatic palm. Yes. His hand trembled a little as he took up the crown and placed it on his brow.

Together, they walked the long aisle. To either side, stable hands and men at arms and seamstresses waved, or smiled as they were able and not a few brushed away tears. As they approached the door, his entourage fell in behind him, his squires before. Conor remained at his side—rather tall and awkward for a nursemaid, but none more loyal. Near the last bed, a small, dark-clad figure knelt laying a poultice on one of the barons. She muttered words in an unknown tongue, not breaking off until she had done. Then she finally faced him. "That last story, Rog, that was something." She bobbed her head. "Can't tell ye how proud I'd be were it true. Or if you even wanted it t'be."

She stayed when she might have left him, she brought aid when she claimed she had none. Roger placed his hand to his forehead, then to his heart, and his mother bent to a curtsey, then returned to her work.

Three servants pushed open the door into dazzling sunshine, and Roger squinted a moment to get used to it. They had set his throne on the broad top step and run a carpet down the rest. A crowd accumulated around the makeshift court, his people, dressed not for royalty, but for work, masons and carpenters with their tools, the children of lords and ladies who now worked alongside them, equally specked in sawdust.

The Hearth Witch's Son

Chaussen made a disapproving grunt, and Roger considered if he'd be better off sending the man to some outer province.

Roger settled gratefully into his throne, and waved a hand for the heralds to bring forward his knights.

The phalanx looked ragged, their armor dented and scored, and more than one missed gauntlet, bracer or greaves. A few helped one another to limp into the yard, and they clumped instead of marching. No matter—they were alive, and among them walked a number of other citizens: carters, farmers and weavers who had taken up arms.

The groom who had wrestled him into submission stepped forward, his eyes glinting white. Of course he had gone; few enough of Roger's people could ride well, but the grooms were among them. The man had the grace to look nervous, mostly, in fact, to look at his feet. Still, he wore the blood of others, and carried a bloody parcel wrapped in cloth.

"Battle was met among the hills, my lord king. We found that these good citizens had prepared to meet the enemy, by the foresight of Lady Rania. They had stores of stones and laid traps of logs or mud. It was slow work, Your Majesty, to separate and confuse the enemy, but it was done at last. And it was she who slew the duke. Cut off his head." He peeled back the cloth from what he carried and displayed the gory prize. A cheer swept the crowd.

"We're having his body brought up on a wagon." As the groom spoke more of the party limped or walked or staggered through the gates, and the flick of Roger's hand sent some of those close by to help them.

"She took him, Your Majesty, but it was not without cost."

His fist clenched he surged to his feet, swaying. The groom stumbled back from Roger's alarm, seeking shelter with the knights, who took him in, the gathering swirling restively. In their midst, a group of them walked close together, and enough of them parted at last to reveal why they moved so slowly. Rania sat in a chair made of their arms, her left leg splinted out in front of her. They carried her forward, and as the others parted away, Roger went limp with relief. Her eyes found him and her lips parted. She pushed against her bearers. "Roger! You're alive."

He could have fainted straight away, and only move-ment stopped it happening, as if he fell in a continuous arc toward her, running down the steps, his arm sliding about her waist, drawing her against him. Her head rested on his shoulder as she wrapped her strong arms around him. "I told you I'd come—I'm so sorry I'm late. I was so afraid you'd not be here when I came home."

Home. To him.

For a long moment, he simply held her, the knights backing off a little way, leaving them balanced in each other's arms. At last he was willing to be parted from her, his retain-ers hovering near, waiting for one or both of them to collapse to the ground.

"Then I did not misjudge," she whispered.

He clenched his fist, and Caterina supplied the translation, then he wiped that away with a curl of his hand. He touched his throat again, the wound that stole his voice, perhaps never to return, and the crown above, and gestured helplessly toward all of those people, the knights who cheered his name and hers, the groom who thought to betray him then rode out with his cavalry, the lowborn and the high, and all of them bearing witness to what shouldn't be.

"Why do you still wear the crown, is that what you're asking? Why are we all still here? You thought it was your voice that held us, or the lies you told on our behalf. My lord king. Many people could have done what you did, raising an army, insisting the tyrant be slain, enforcing justice in truth and not merely in name. It doesn't change the fact that nobody did, until you." She cupped his face with one hand, the other still wrapped to his shoulders, keeping them both from falling. "Many could have done what you did, Roger, but nobody could have been who you are."

"Your hand is a gift, my love, royal, or no; magic, or no. It isn't your stories we're following, it's you." She stroked his temple, his cheek, her thumb across his lips, then she whispered, "Honest and true."

If you enjoyed this book, I would appreciate if you took the time to rate or review it wherever you share books! Your reviews really can make a difference to an author.

Have you read the other Tales of Bladesend?

Winning the Gallows Field

In spite of Trelayne's victories in battle, the road home is longer than the young knight ever imagined, and it must begin with rejecting his peasant companion, Derik, and denying the memory of the half-orc companion who gave his life for them. Forced to admit that the battle has changed him, Trelayne tries to be the champion for the peasantry, only to make things worse—Derik imprisoned, his betrothed rejecting him, his war-wounds throbbing. Honor provokes him to claim a duel with the swordmaster in the hopes of earning Derik's freedom, but the veterans find that winning a battle is not the same as winning a war—and not all demons wear an ugly face.

Joenna's Ax

After Joenna's half-orc son is killed in battle, she disguises herself as a man to join the army and avenge him, adding one notch to the handle of her ax for every demons she kills. But when she volunteers to lead a suicide charge of half-orc scouts, she risks her secret and her own mission to try to save them. Rewarded for her prowess with a grant of land and ownership of her half-orc man-at-arms, Joenna plots to rescue all of the half-orcs from the king's plan to destroy these reviled bastards—making herself a traitor along with them. When their haven is discovered, Joenna leads the half-orcs in a desperate fight against a famous warrior and his knights in the hopes of winning their freedom and claiming their humanity.

More books by this author

The Singer's Legacy series

The Singer's Crown

When his uncle murders his family to take the throne, Prince Kattanan DuRhys is the only royal left alive… at a terrible cost. Stripped of his manhood, Kattanan travels as a court singer from one wealthy patron to the next. Given as a courtship gift to the young Princess Melisande, Kattanan feels the stirring of emotions he thought were denied him. But her jealous fiancée has other plans—and the sinister magic to carry them out.

Must Kattanan sacrifice his song to win his kingdom, and the woman he loves?

The Eunuch's Heir

Prince Wolfram of Lochalyn can't possibly live up to the reputation of his father, the Blessed Rhys, so why bother to try? Until a series of self-started catastrophes plunges him into the midst of the growing refugee population. They claim to be fleeing a war, and only Wolfram sees the danger that lurks in their mysterious ways. But his love for an exotic stranger, and his concern for the princess who pursues him collide with a more terrible struggle, in which his kingdom may fall and his very Goddess be brought to Her knees. Discredited by his past and disdained by his own mother, Wolfram must find the truth of his birth, and fight to make amends for all that he's done—or be seduced by the darkness of distant power.

The Bastard Queen

Beloved bastard of an unloved king, Fiona will do almost anything to please her father, even studying magic though she never shows more than a spark of talent. But the plague that grips their city sends her to work with the dying, as enmity builds between the two peoples her father has brought together. When arson burns a hospital, everyone blames the growing racial tension, until an unexpected suspect comes from the woods on a spirit-quest destined to uncover the secrets of Fiona's past. Then Reynaud, long Fiona's suitor, suddenly asks to marry her sister. Struggling to find a cure for the plague, Fiona becomes ever more convinced that its emer-gence is no coincidence—and that Reynaud may be leading a conspiracy that will end in genocide.

About the Author

Elaine Isaak writes knowledge inspired adventure fiction including *The Singer's Legacy* fantasy series, *The Dark Apostle* series about medieval surgery as by E. C. Ambrose, and the Bone Guard international thrillers as by E. Chris Ambrose. Her latest releases are *Bone Guard Two: The Nazi Skull*, and *The King of Next Week*, from Guardbridge Books. Her short stories have appeared in *Fireside*, *Warrior Women* and *Fantasy for the Throne*, among many others, and she has edited several volumes of New Hampshire Pulp Fiction. Elaine has taught at the Odyssey Writing Workshop, as well as at conventions and writer's groups across the country, and judged writing competitions from New Hampshire Literary Idol to the World Fantasy Award.

Elaine dropped out of art school to found her own business. A former professional costumer and soft sculpture creator, Elaine now works as a part-time adventure guide. In addition to writing, Elaine creates wearable art employing weaving, dyeing and felting into her unique garments. To learn about all of her writing, check out RocinanteBooks.com

Find her at https://www.facebook.com/elaine.isaak.7 or twitter @ElaineIsaak and @ecambroseauthor

www.ingramcontent.com/pod-product-compliance
Lightning Source LLC
Chambersburg PA
CBHW050900180626
46814CB00007B/2807